NIKI'S HONOR

LAILA ANWARZAI AYOUBI

First Edition

PAGE PUBLISHING, INC.
New York, NY

First originally published by Page Publishing, Inc. 2015

ISBN 978-1-63417-914-0 (pbk)
ISBN 978-1-63417-915-7 (digital)

Printed in the United States of America

Author's Note

In my Women's Resistance course at Butler University, I discussed chapter 8, "Murder of Women," from *The Penguin Atlas of Women in the World*. One section of the book described *honor killing*, a term used to identify a form of legally or socially sanctioned revenge exercised within a family against a female who is deemed to have soiled the family's honor, usually through behavior that is judged as sexually inappropriate.

At the end of that chapter, there is a world map with different colors highlighting the countries that practice honor killings. In countries marked with dark purple, honor killings occur more frequently. The dark purple covers Bangladesh, India, Pakistan, and Afghanistan; these marks extend to all the Arab countries, a few countries in Europe (including Italy), and even to Brazil and Ecuador.

My students asked me about the honor killing culture in Afghanistan, my native country. To be honest, while living in Afghanistan, I had heard the term, but I do not recall a story about it; or if I had heard a story, I did not fully absorb it or understand the relation of it with honor killing. Their question evoked my curiosity.

I shared my class discussion with some of my relatives and asked if they knew anything about the honor killing culture in Afghanistan. The answers were sort of conflicting—from complete denial to factual stories. According to one elder family member, honor killings occur in Afghanistan rarely even though this terrifying culture has existed for a long time among some people. One of these horrifying stories is about Niki, a young girl in the village of Angur Dara.

In addition to Niki's story, I have included a few more episodes related to the topic. These stories show that not all Afghan women are oppressed. Many Afghan women have been decision makers and have held high positions within their families, but still they have been prisoners of their ever-present culture. The honor killing practices are condemnable and are the actions of a few extremist people and does not reflect the Afghan people as a whole.

My purpose in writing this book is to enlighten people and to stop these horrifying practices. It is my desire that all people and cultures become more humane and exercise the utmost kindness and love toward their girls and women.

Laila Anwarzai Ayoubi, PhD
April 11, 2013

Acknowledgment

While writing this novel, I received support, motivation and encouragement from many people who graciously offered their insights, knowledge and editing skills to me. Their efforts are indeed reflected in this book and I am greatly indebted to them.

I begin, however, by acknowledging and thanking my family and particularly my husband, Bashir, and our sons - Ali, Edris and Slaimon - for their unwavering and total support. I thank my late mentor and teacher, Martin University Professor William York, for providing invaluable advice and guidance to me.

I also thank all my friends and especially Kathy Gannon, bureau chief/international correspondent, *Associated Press*, who encouraged and motivated me from the very beginning to write this book. I thank as well all those persons who wish to remain anonymous for their many contributions. In conclusion, I thank the Honorable Mark S. Froehlich, a retired judge, for his proof reading and editing expertise. Without his support this novel may not have been completed.

To my sister Fauzia.

Prologue

The young father, in private, asked his wife Ozra to name their newborn girl Niki. In Pashto and Farsi, *Niki* means "goodness." In villages, it was embarrassing for a young man to choose a name for his newborn daughter.

The family lived in a small house in the same neighborhood as Ozra's parents. Ozra's husband loved to take his wife and daughter to picnics in the vineyards and orchards on the outskirts of their village. He also took them to the city, Kabul, and to its parks, ice cream stores, and especially to the homes of Ozra's relatives.

Niki was about three years old when her father died. Ozra and her daughter moved to her parents' home. Ozra's parents were not rich, but they were very kind and well respected in their village. They were also related to the Khan's tribe.

It was a tradition during Eids, the Muslim holidays, for villagers and relatives to go to the Khan's house to show respect. On those days, Niki eagerly accompanied her mother and her grandparents. There she played with many children and the Khan's wife would give gifts to them.

When Niki was six years old, her grandparents died. She and her mother moved to her Uncle Azeem's house. Her uncle's wife, Nassima, was considered a vicious woman by many of the villagers.

Ozra continued the tradition of going with her daughter to the Khan's house during these religious holidays. Niki was eight years old the last time she went. On these visits, Niki joined the other children and played in the courtyard while her mother went inside to talk with the other women.

As always, the Khan's wife, Shah Gul, appeared on the porch with a bag full of candies and coins: Eid gifts for the children.

The children eagerly ran toward her with happy shouts.

"Come one at a time. Tell me your name and your mother's name," she instructed them.

Her loud, bossy voice quieted the children. They stood in silence in front of her. It was this year, among all the children, that Shah Gul noticed a little girl with fairy tale beauty. She was the only child who, after receiving her Eid gift, kissed Shah Gul's hands expressing appreciation and respect.

"Tell me, again, your name and your mother's name," Shah Gul demanded.

"I am Niki, daughter of Ozra," she said, and then quickly ran to join the other children, all the while happily gazing at her gifts.

The beautiful face and good manners of this little girl stayed in Shah Gul's mind. After the Eid, Shah Gul sent a message to Ozra that she wanted to see her. Without questioning the request, Ozra promptly went to the Kahn's house to see Shah Gul.

It was at this visit, that Shah Gul asked Ozra's consent to engage Niki, now only nine years old, to her son, Nur Gul, who was fifteen years old. It was a common custom to engage children. The young girl would stay in her parents' house until reaching the proper age to be wed. For Ozra, a dream had come true.

Ozra immediately gave her consent, and told Shah Gul, "It is an honor that the son of a Khan will someday marry my daughter."

Shah Gul was known for being arrogant. Even when she had asked for Niki's engagement, she expressed this haughtiness. "There is a saying," she explained, "when people in our status find a girl for marriage to their sons, they consider two things: a girl who has a well-known father, or a girl with extraordinary beauty."

Ozra felt disappointed that Niki did not have a well-known father. But looking at Shah Gul, one could clearly see that, "Shah Gul must have had a well-known father!"

"When Niki reaches the age of seventeen, I will make the arrangements for a spectacular wedding that everybody will remember for a long time," Shah Gul added.

The engagement party was planned for a Friday, two weeks later.

Chapter 1

The engagement party took place on a beautiful spring day in the house of Ozra's brother-in-law. That morning, since the weather was very pleasant and warm, Shah Gul and her companions walked together to the celebration. Shah Gul, even though very heavyset, tried to walk at the same pace as the others, but with much difficulty. Her face became covered in sweat. She kept wiping it with a handkerchief, which quickly became soaked and barely usable.

As they walked along, two women, relatives of Shah Gul, sang special songs for the occasion, praising the beauty of the bride-to-be and the bravery of the groom-to-be, beating hard with their palms on their tambourines.

The women followed young boys, who were carrying on their heads oversized trays full of sweets, clothing, and accessories for Niki. For the engagement party, it was common to bring gifts on such trays, called *khuncha*, which were made of thin wood covered with colorful, glossy fabrics.

The small well-dressed group entered the rough and dirty alley, which was lined with shabby small houses on each side. Many girls and women residents of the alley were up on their rooftops, waiting to see the wealthy guests bringing the engagement gifts for Ozra's beautiful daughter.

Some of the young girls looking down were counting the trays, wishing that one day somebody would bring them engagement gifts like these. A few even bet that the heavy woman was the mother-in-law because she walked funny. With each step to the left or to the right, her whole body leaned that way, causing the observing girls to laugh.

When the guests arrived, Niki was playing in the courtyard and singing with her friends, "*Koo koo koo, barguee chenar.*" It is a Persian little girl's play song, which Niki had learned from her relatives in Kabul, and had taught to her Pashto-speaking friends in the village.

The simple play song came from a short story: "Pigeons are coming to a river where girls are sitting under the willow trees and eating pomegranates." The girls made a circle, held hands, and joyfully sang, "*Koo koo koo, barguee chenar, doukhtara shishta qatar, mikhorand dana anar* . . . " They stepped forward and made the circle smaller, and then they stepped backward and made it bigger.

Shah Gul called for Niki so she could get her dressed for the occasion. Ozra and a few other women followed them into a humble small room to help. The engagement dress selected by Shah Gul was pink velvet with golden tiny flowers, including a white satin shalwar, a small pink chiffon veil with a golden silk margin, and a pair of shiny white shoes.

After dressing Niki, Shah Gul said, "For the wedding, I will give her my *chamkaly,* that old styled Afghani necklace that belonged to my grandmother. And I will give them a big wedding that this village will remember—forever."

Ozra told Shah Gul, "Your words take me into a daydream. I see my daughter in her wedding dress with a gold necklace, looking like a fairy tale bride in the ancient tales."

"I chose the beauty of the world, a perfect match for my handsome son. Their wedding will fulfill my wishes. They will bring handsome sons into the world!" Shah Gul was talking excitedly while holding Niki's chin up and looking at her beautifully shaped hazel green eyes.

Shah Gul said to Niki, "Look, those trays full of gifts and sweets are for you—all of them!"

Niki had no idea what was going on. She told her mother that she wanted to join the other girls playing in the courtyard.

Her mother explained to her, "We are celebrating your engagement to Nur Gul. When you grow older, you will marry him and then move to their big house. You will then always have good food and nice dresses."

Niki asked, "After the party, will I still be able to play with my friends?"

"No! Starting today, you are engaged to the Khan's son, and it does not look good that people see you in the alley playing with other children. Now it is time for you to learn about housework," Ozra said and continued, "Now sit still. I have work to do."

For the guests, Ozra had furnished a side of the courtyard with worn-out cheap carpets, mattresses, and nonmatching cushions.

Shah Gul's guests were dressed in expensive clothes, but their makeup styles were the same as Ozra's guests—white chalk-colored powder on their faces, hot red lipstick, and hot pink-colored circles on their cheeks. They used *surma*, a charcoal-colored powder, grounded from natural black stones, on their eyebrows, and drew lines around their eyes.

The women were singing, dancing, and showing off their new dresses and their typical village-style jewelry. The sharp odor of the perfume used by the village women was in the air and became stronger the more they danced.

At last, the guests sat down for the engagement ceremony. Shah Gul and the other women in the room came out and joined the guests. She occupied an entire mattress herself and also helped herself to a few more cushions for her back and elbows. She had Niki sit next to her.

Ozra had fixed a small tray full of sweets for Shah Gul. This was a sign of consent from the girl's family making the engagement official. The tray was called *qhand wa destmal,* and it was full of traditional Afghan sugarcoated almonds called *nukle*. These almonds, however, were shapeless showing a lower quality. There were also two sugar cones wrapped in golden-colored foil. The tray was covered with a silky scarf, which had cheap tassels on the corners.

"If I had the money, I would have bought gold tassels as Safia Jan did for her older daughter, Nasrin's, engagement." Ozra was referring to her relatives in Kabul, whose younger daughter, Roya, was the same age as Niki. They were now out of the country, and like Ozra would have been well pleased with Niki's engagement party.

Next, Ozra carried the tray carefully across the room and placed it in front of Shah Gul. At that moment, the other women started to sing a congratulatory song in Pashto: "*Mubarak dee sha, Mubarak dee sha.*"

Ozra, after placing the tray down, kissed Shah Gul's hand. Shah Gul then kissed Ozra's face, turned, and kissed Niki on both cheeks.

The women continued to dance and sing. The lunch, prepared at Shah Gul's house, was brought out. It was enough for all the women of the alley. The main dish was brown rice with lamb, with side dishes of meatballs, potatoes, spinach, and breads. The aroma was delightful.

The poor women and children of the alley, always ready for a celebration, came with their containers to get food. They stood or sat on the bare ground in the courtyard, watching the rich guests with amazement.

Ozra's sister-in-law, Nassima, hated Ozra, and was always trying to please Shah Gul. She kept running back and forth, offering tea and drinks to Shah Gul, hoping that she would engage one of her daughters to marry her younger son Zalmai.

That day, Nur Gul, who was wearing an Afghani embroidered white *shelwar kamis*, accompanied his father, Hajji Khan, to the mosque for the Friday prayer. After the prayer, Hajji Khan announced his son's early engagement. The *mullah* and the village men who were at the mosque congratulated him, saying, "You are a good man to take care of that orphan girl."

Later, Shah Gul told her husband, "I am very happy with my choice, but if Niki's widowed mother remarries, it would damage our reputation because remarrying a widow is embarrassing, with Niki still living with her mother until she reaches the marriage age."

Ozra had a very hard life living at the house of her brother-in-law, who was a good man, but whose wife treated Ozra as though she were her slave.

***

A while later, in a gathering, two old women, Bibi Shirin and Babo, had a conversation. During their conversations, Bibi Shirin talked about her niece Ozra, and Babo spoke about her son Baz Gul.

"My poor niece has a hard time living in the house of her brother-in-law. I wish someone good would come along and marry her," Ozra's aunt told her friend. Babo lived in Sheen Klay not far from Angur Dara.

"I am looking for another wife for my son, Baz Gul. What if Ozra would marry him?" Babo asked.

The old women continued talking more about this between themselves. The next day, Bibi Shrin went to see Ozra and told her their plan. Ozra, although she was having a miserable life, did not accept the idea of remarriage. She was afraid it would bring Niki's status down. The engagement of Niki to the Khan's son gave Niki a prestige among the other girls, which was most important.

Bibi Shrin, who admired Ozra's love and sacrifice for her daughter, said, "I just want you to have a comfortable life with Niki. Baz Gul's mother will treat you well. She is a good woman. Other news I have for you: Safia Jan is back from abroad. Last week, I was in her house. She asked about you. Go visit her."

Bibi Shrin left, feeling very worried about Ozra.

After Niki's engagement to the Khan's son, Nassima had taken on a deeper grudge against Ozra and Niki. She tried to find ways to hurt them. It started when she refused to give them permission to go to their relatives' house in Kabul. One day, she threw a pot full of hot soup at Ozra which burned her legs, blaming her for making the soup too salty. Then she rationed their food: only one portion for both of them. Ozra always shared her food with Niki, while staying hungry herself most of the time.

The torments continued daily. Ozra cursed the custom requiring widows to live with either her parents or with her husband's family. She wished to be free and go work someplace else to support herself and Niki. However, she was a prisoner of the custom. Ozra endured all the punishments and humiliations, until one day she overheard a conversation between Nassima and her best friend, which gave her goosebumps. Ozra was on her way to serve them tea and was just behind the door, with a tray in her hand, when she heard them talking.

"You know how much I despise Ozra and her daughter, who is the fiancée of the Khan's son. At the engagement party, I envied her so much, especially since Shah Gul said that she is going to give Niki her *chamkaly*. You remember that *chamkaly*? Her famous *chamkaly* that she wears especially during Eids. Oh, how much I want to deform Niki's face," the sister-in-law said, grinding her teeth.

"Then do it! When her mother is not around, and she is asleep, pour a small amount of acid on her cheeks. They would blame it on the sting of a scorpion, which is not something unusual in our village," the friend said.

"I do not have acid," Nassima said.

Her friend said, "Hold on, I remember something else! I know a woman in another town who sells the root of a special tree, which makes people lose their minds. I will bring it for you to boil and then give it to Niki. After a few days, she'll become crazy!"

"I want to see Niki become ugly and crazy," the sister-in-law said. Both of them laughed loudly and acted crazy themselves for a moment.

Ozra, shocked by what she had heard, pulled herself together and entered the room. She patiently served the tea even though her heart was pounding and her mind was still full of their evil deeds. She was extremely worried about the safety of her innocent, beautiful daughter, Niki.

Nassima, after that conversation with her friend, changed her attitude toward Ozra and Niki. She even started to act kindly to them. A few days later, Ozra took advantage of this attitude change and asked for permission to visit her relatives in Kabul.

Nassima, still devising her plan to harm Niki, happily gave them permission to go. Ozra quickly got herself and Niki ready, afraid that Nassima might change her mind.

Ozra thanked Allah for having kind relatives in Kabul. Safia and her husband, Habib, belonged to the Angur Dara Khan's tribe. Safia was Ozra's father's cousin who lived in Kabul.

They headed out of the house. On the way, Ozra walked fast and Niki ran next to her. Ozra was crying under her burqa.

"Mother, are you crying?" Niki asked.

"Why should I cry? I am happy to go and visit our relatives. Oh, before we leave for Kabul, I need to stop at my old Aunt Bibi Shrin's house," Ozra said. Once there, Ozra privately told her aunt that she had agreed to marry Baz Gul. They then spent a long time discussing the marriage. Afterward, the mother and daughter went to Kabul.

Safia was happy to see them but noticed deep signs of worry on Ozra's face. She kept quiet until Niki went to Roya's room. Then Safia asked Ozra, "Sister, what is wrong?"

Ozra, who never complained about her life, broke into tears and told Safia about her sister-in-law's plans to harm Niki. After a pause, with embarrassment, she told her of the plan to marry the suitor that her old aunt had found for her.

"I will marry to save Niki. What is your advice for me?" she asked.

"Do what you think is best for you," Safia advised her, and added, "leave Niki with us for as long as you want."

Ozra returned home without Niki. She told her sister-in-law that Niki had become very sick and Safia would take her to a doctor. The relatives in Kabul loved Niki like their own child.

With a kind tone, Nassima said, "It is not good to leave a little girl in a relative's house. They are not your sisters or brothers. You have to bring her back. Here is her house."

In a few days, Baz Gul's mother sent some older relatives to speak with Ozra's brother-in-law to get his permission for Ozra to remarry.

Azeem, the brother-in-law, who was greatly troubled at seeing his sister-in-law and his niece living in his dark and smoky kitchen and working as servants for his wife, immediately gave his consent.

Nassima became upset at losing her servants. She tried to convince her husband to change his mind and said, "Where is your honor, to let your brother's widow marry a stranger? People will laugh at you. It is not in our custom to let a widow remarry!"

Azeem earnestly responded to his wife, "In Islam, a widow is free and has the right to remarry. Or, as it is our custom, I will not let her marry outside of the family. I will marry her myself! I cannot keep a young woman as a slave in my kitchen for the rest of her life. She is twenty-eight years old! I have given my consent that she may remarry whomever she wants. Let people laugh at me. I am not a Khan! I am a nobody!"

"But you are from a Khan's descent," she said.

"But I am poor and considered nobody. I can marry Ozra because she is my brother's widow, can't I?" he asked.

After listening to her husband, Nassima remained silent and even forgot her heinous plan to injure Niki. She wanted Ozra and Niki to get lost as soon as possible. She did not want her husband to have another wife.

Ozra and Niki soon went to stay with Aunt Bibi Shirin until Ozra remarried.

Her marriage was a simple *nikah*, performed by their local *mullah*, in the presence of her two male cousins as witnesses. Baz Gul's mother, as the custom, brought food and sweets for the ceremony.

Afterward, Ozra kissed Bibi Shirin's hands to say good-bye, before moving to Sheen Klay Village. She put on her burqa, took Niki's hand, and followed Babo, her new mother-in-law, out to where a taxi was waiting. They got in the taxi and waited for Baz Gul to bring out her belongings.

Baz Gul soon came out carrying a heavy wooden trunk and a silver-colored steel one. He carried them easily as if they were not heavy at all. He was in his early forties, tall, muscular, and well-built.

Ozra, from behind her burqa, attentively observed him. He was wearing a new white shelwar kamize. The front top part of his shirt was embroidered delicately, and he wore a light brown turban. He seemed very good-looking to her.

He entered the taxi. They drove away leaving the village children running and shouting their farewells in the cloud of dust left behind. In the taxi, no one spoke. It was quiet except for the sound of the rubber tires on the uneven road and the hum of the old but dependable engine.

Ozra remembered the old days when her first husband took her and Niki to picnics in the village vineyards and orchards. She remembered the trips to Kabul and its parks and ice cream stores and the visits with relatives.

She also remembered the bad days, after her husband died and when both her parents died, when she moved to the house of her brother-in-law. She remembered only too well those cold days outside when she washed piles of dirty clothes, pulled water from the well, and heated the water in the courtyard. Sometimes when the wood was wet, she struggled to light a fire. She also recalled collecting animal dung, which she placed in a corner of the stable to dry, before using as fuel.

The taxi, barely slowing down, suddenly stopped, interrupting her thoughts. The taxi came to a halt in front of a small old house in the alley. The entrance gate, smaller than the neighbors' gates, was made of thick wood, but like the larger gates of the neighborhood, it had a heavy metal latch, showing the great skill of the village blacksmith, when it had been made decades ago. The gate opened onto a small treeless courtyard.

Across from the gate, there were a few rooms, next to each other, made of thick mud walls with small windows. Next to the gate, on the right, was a smaller house, where an old uncle and his wife lived. All the doors and window frames had faded blue paint on them.

The old uncle and his wife had prepared food, and they were waiting for Baz Gul, Babo, Ozra, and Niki when they arrived. This small gathering of relatives celebrated the wedding that evening.

Babo was happy to find a second wife for her son. Ozra was a good woman, and Babo looked forward to sharing her room with Niki.

During the summers, Baz Gul assisted his uncle, working on an inherited small plot of land in Sheen Klay Village. He spent the rest of the year with his first wife and two daughters in a small village in Baghlan Province, in the north of Afghanistan, working in the local sugar factory.

Ozra, before the wedding, agreed to the condition of being a second wife. She and Niki soon found a peaceful life in their new home. Everything was working out as best as possible for the mother and daughter.

Many years before, while doing military service in Baghlan, Baz Gul had fallen in love with an Uzbek girl and married her, but under one condition—she would never move to Sheen Klay Village. She was the only child of her family, and her father let her live at his house after her wedding, as was her wish. When he was not working on his land in Sheen Klay, Baz Gul lived with her there.

After marrying Ozra, Baz Gul continued his regular life of commuting back and forth to both places.

Ozra was happy living with her mother-in-law, who gave her the responsibilities of the house. They both appreciated and understood each other. But most importantly, there was now a safe haven for Niki. Ozra was skillful in embroidery and made bedspreads, tablecloths, and napkins to sell. From the money she earned, she was able to keep a decent household, so as not to be embarrassed when relatives came to visit, especially Shah Gul, who accepted Ozra's situation.

After a few years, Baz Gul's mother died. However, Ozra and Niki were not alone on the property, as the older aunt and uncle were still living there.

Often, when Baz Gul was out of the village, Ozra took Niki to visit relatives in Kabul. Those visits helped Niki learn the city's culture and to speak Dari as well.

***

Shah Gul and her son, Nur Gul, continued to bring and send gifts to Niki for the holidays, as it was the custom to bring or send gifts to the fiancée.

Nur Gul was among the few boys from the village, who, after finishing the *madrassa,* the religious school in the village mosque, went to high school and then to the Teacher's Institute in Kabul.

When Baz Gul was out of town, Nur Gul had to come more often to Sheen Klay Village to check on mother and daughter and run errands for them. Nur Gul, a good-looking, tall, slim young man, was no stranger in the alley where Ozra lived.

In the villages, it was not common for betrothed couples to see each other before the *nikah,* the religious marriage, unless they performed the *nikah* during the engagement period. For honor's sake, Shah Gul and Ozra thought that performing *nikah* would be necessary in order for Nur Gul to come and go freely to Ozra's house.

Also, if there is no son in the family, the future son-in-law could take on some responsibilities. Therefore, performing *nikah* would be necessary, so they soon performed the *nikah.*

The respectful behavior of Nur Gul allowed him the opportunity to come and visit his fiancée very often. During these visits, Nur Gul and Niki became good friends, and gained confidence and trust in each other. Nur Gul talked about his studies with Niki and his wish to get a scholarship to go abroad for more education.

"What is a scholarship?" Niki asked when Nur Gul was talking about school one day.

Nur Gul replied, "It is an opportunity for good students to go abroad and study more. When they return, they will get promotions and earn more money. My wish is to get a scholarship and go to India, which is close to our country, and I would like to learn English."

Nur Gul was a bright and hardworking student at the Teacher's Institute in Kabul, and he did receive what he had so earnestly worked to obtain—a scholarship to go to India.

"The program is for two years, but I signed up to not take summer breaks and will finish my studies in fourteen months," Nur Gul said to comfort Niki.

Nur Gul left for India and remained there for the required fourteen months. When it was Eids, Shah Gul brought gifts to Niki from her son. At those times, the future mother-in-law talked with Niki about preparations for her son's spectacular wedding. She counted the months and said, "Next year, in the fall, after the harvest, we will have our wedding."

Chapter 2

Seven years had passed since Ozra and Niki had moved to Sheen Klay Village. Niki, now sixteen years old, had grown into a very beautiful girl making her very popular among relatives and friends.

One of Niki's best friends was Shinky, who lived along the same alley as Niki. That fall, among many other weddings, Shinky's parents planned one for her.

A week before the wedding, Shinky's family had a gathering for the relatives and friends to help with the preparation of the dowry. It was a sunny day in mid-August, a perfect day for the gathering in the courtyard.

Ozra wanted to leave early to help. When she was leaving, she called out to her daughter, "Niki, finish your chores and join me at the party. We will return early because tonight Baz Gul might return from Baghlan."

Ozra called out to her daughter one more time, saying, "Come lock the gate because the uncle and his wife went to visit their daughter. Nobody is in the house."

"I will lock the gate, just let me take the dishes to the kitchen first," replied Niki from the house. On the way to the kitchen, she was thinking about what to wear to Shinky's party.

She forgot to lock the gate.

After she finished her chores around the house, she thought, *Now, it is time for me to prepare myself for the party*! She went to her room and turned on the small transistor radio, the only sign of modern technology in the house. It was a gift from Safia to Ozra, in return for an embroidered bedspread.

The radio was broadcasting one of her favorite Pashto folk songs. She hummed along. "Go to Nangharhar Province, in the east of Afghanistan, and bring me a black dress with three or four fresh flowers." Pashtun girls and women in Afghanistan loved to wear black dresses decorated with silver paisleys and coins.

"What should I wear?" Niki asked herself as she walked to her trunk. She opened it and chose the dress that her mother-in-law had brought her at the last Eid. She placed it on top of the trunk, took her bath container and radio, and walked to the bathroom.

She placed the radio on the small wooden shelf near the bath and the container on the floor. Inside the container were many things, including her favorite pink and green-colored scented soaps that her fiancé had brought her from Kabul.

In the bathroom's fireplace, she made a fire to heat water and soaked a special mud for her hair. This mixture is known as *gueeli sar shore,* which is a brown claylike hard mud. She loved to use this natural product to make her hair more silky and shiny. For the hard mud to become soft and look creamy, it needed to be soaked with water for a little while. While she was waiting for the *gueeli sar shore* to become soft, she undid her hair's many braids.

The bathroom became steamy, was half-dark, and only a tiny window near the ceiling let a narrow strip of light sneak through.

Niki undressed and started her bath by putting the mud on her hair and scrubbing her feet and hands. After a few minutes, she rubbed and rinsed her hair clean. She stood upright to soap her body. She loved to see the bubbles and smell the soap's aroma. As she lathered her body and thought about her wedding day, which was planned exactly one year from that day, she didn't realize, with the radio playing so loud, that the front gate had been opened. She was in her own world and never heard the creaking, clinking noise that it made.

Baz Gul entered his house unnoticed.

"Niki must be deaf. She always has the radio so loud," he said as he walked into the small hallway.

Since nobody was home, Niki had left the bathroom door fully open. In the steam-filled bathing room, with the pleasant scent of soap in the air, she felt relaxed, washing herself while listening to the music.

Baz Gul was on his way down the hallway to his room, thinking his wife might be around, when he suddenly stopped in front of the bathroom.

He whispered, "I cannot believe my eyes. Is this Niki? She looks like a grown woman." Then he said, "I should not look! I raised her as my own daughter!"

Baz Gul, feeling ashamed to be standing there, turned his head and walked quickly toward his room, but his mind was on that scent-filled bath, and the vision of beauty he saw there.

Baz Gul began thinking about a saying that a *mullah* had once said at the mosque: "*Hoors* are in paradise! The most beautiful girls are rewards for men who behave well on earth." He couldn't get that thought out of his mind.

"I am seeing a *Hoor*? *Toba toba* (repent, repent)! I am as her father, I am as her father . . . ," he kept saying. "I am as her father, I am as her father."

He walked back and forth to and from his room before heading back to the steamy bath. He became overwhelmed with desire. Finally, he paused at the door.

The door of the bathroom looked like a frame for an extraordinary picture of a beautiful young naked girl. The sight froze Baz Gul. His desire grew even stronger. He entered the bathroom.

"Baba Baz Gul, it is me, Niki!" she said while hurriedly trying to grab a towel to cover up her nakedness. Baz Gul threw his large turban to the floor, picked up the frightened girl like a small helpless bird with his large hands, carrying her to her own bedroom, and dropped her on the mattress. Niki felt that lightning had hit her, and like a little bird, she was struggling with all her strength to get away—but Baz Gul was too strong, too big, and too heavy.

The last thing she remembered was Baba Baz Gul forcing himself on top of her. She felt that her bones were being crushed by his weight. She went unconscious. Baz Gul did not even notice.

He left the house while Niki was lying helplessly on the soiled bed. Her thighs were covered with blood, and she no longer smelled of scented soap.

When Niki regained consciousness, she felt sharp pain all over her numb body. She soon realized what had happened. Still in shock and fully disoriented, she managed to crawl to the bathroom to wash off the blood.

She told herself, "My mother will have a heart attack if she learns what Baz Gul did to me. She can never know, and I vow that she will never know."

It took her some time to clean herself up and fully regain her senses. When she was done, she left the house. She stumbled down the narrow alley to Shinky's house, a few doors away. The destination, it seemed, would never be reached.

It was a sunny day with large thick clouds scattered in the sky here and there. The fresh air, however, felt suffocating to her. She kept walking until she reached her friend's house for the party.

When her mother saw her, she was alarmed and asked, "Why is your face so pale? Are you having your period?" Niki's mother did not wait for her to respond but turned to Shinky's mother and said, "She has a painful period."

"Mother, do not talk about my period, it is embarrassing. I am fine," Niki whispered.

At the party, some girls were singing and dancing, while others helped with arranging and placing the clothes and accessories on the large wooden trays. Some women were busy making dough for the pastries and fixing food for the guests.

"The dough is ready . . . I need help making cookies and putting designs on them," yelled a middle-aged woman who was squatting in a corner with a large clay dish full of sweet dough in front of her. A few girls answered the call and walked over to help. Niki also went to help with the cookie designs.

"No, Niki, come sing and dance with us. You dance very well, and your dress is very pretty," one of her friends said while pulling her arm to get her to dance.

At that moment, Niki had no desire to dance. She told her friend, "I will join you later. Let me help her, I love to design cookies." The friend let her arm go and rejoined the dancing group. All the girls were full of life—dancing, singing, and laughing. None of them noticed Niki's pain.

At the end of the party, mother and daughter walked back home.

Ozra became impatient with her daughter's slow walking and said, "You are dragging yourself! It looks like you did not eat. Walk faster."

Niki obeyed and forced herself to walk faster.

That night, Baz Gul did not come home. It happened more and more often that Baz Gul did not come home on the days he said he would.

A few days after the assault, Baz Gul sent someone to Ozra to tell her that the sugar factory had finally hired him full time. He would stay in Baghlan. He sent her some money with the messenger.

Ozra told Niki, "My heart was telling me that one day he would return permanently to his first wife and his daughters. He married me to serve his mother. I am grateful that she was a good woman. I have you, and you are my world." She started to cry and cursed her destiny.

Ozra continued to live in Baz Gul's house with Niki. Skillful in embroidery, Ozra was taking in more orders to prepare a humble dowry for her daughter and to take care of some expenses. She also did work for Safia and other relatives in Kabul. They loved this mother and her daughter.

In the next few months, when Ozra went to Kabul, Niki wanted to stay home with the old aunt and uncle. Her mother was surprised at her sudden loss of interest in going to visit Roya, who was her best friend from childhood.

Chapter 3

During the past six months, nobody noticed Niki's belly since it was the cold season and she was wearing a shawl over her clothes. She did not have any noticeable pregnancy sickness. However, there was no easy way to hide her growing belly.

One day, Ozra focused her eyes on Niki, crunched her face, and in a moaning voice asked, "What am I seeing? Are you . . . I am not able to say that you are pregnant. Tell me what is going on?"

When she saw Niki's pale face and pleading eyes, Ozra fainted. Niki splashed water on her mother's face, put her head on her lap, and started to weep.

Ozra thought that Nur Gul, Niki's fiancé, had come and slept with Niki, and she was too embarrassed to tell her mother what had really happened. Getting pregnant during the engagement was taboo. Neither mother nor daughter knew what to do.

A visit from Aunt Nazo, an older woman who loved to gossip, created yet another problem. It was a cold winter day when she came to visit Ozra and Niki. Both mother and daughter did not want to see any visitors at all at this time.

Ozra thought, *It is not noble not to invite a guest inside the home, even when that person loves to gossip with exaggeration.* She remembered the expression about those people who love to exaggerate:

"When they see one crow, they would say they saw forty crows." Nazo was one of those people.

Nonetheless, Ozra invited the unexpected guest into their home and walked her to the room with the *sandaly*, a type of heater. The *sandaly* was a low square table with a large quilt on top. Under the table was a steel dish with well-burned charcoals, covered with ashes, to make the heat last longer. People could sit or sleep around the *sandaly*, under the quilt.

While walking to the room, Ozra said, "Niki is not feeling well."

Niki was lying under the quilt of the *sandaly*. She tried to get up to greet the elder relative.

"Do not get up, my daughter, your mother said that you are not feeling well," she said. Instead she went to her, sat beside her, and kissed her forehead.

She then took her burqa off, giving it to Ozra to hang on a wooden peg on the wall. Ozra offered her a place to sit under the *sandaly*. Then she went to the kitchen to finish cooking lunch.

Nazo, who had a thick veil on her head, sneezed many times and coughed constantly. With a wrinkled handkerchief, she cleaned her watery eyes and nose. She was a big woman with a reddish face and thick, long, almost connected eyebrows.

As soon as she sat, she told Niki, "Your forehead was not hot. That means you are not sick. Staying under the quilt makes you lazy." Jokingly, Nazo added, "You are spoiled because you are the fiancée of Nur Gul, the son of the Khan!"

She scolded her saying, "It is not good that a mother works in the kitchen and her daughter lies under the *sandaly*."

Finally, with a firm voice, she commanded, "Get up and bring your old aunt a cup of tea with lots of *gur*." (*Gur* is a sweet substance made from sugar cane).

The commanding voice of Aunt Nazo made Niki get up and walk to the kitchen. She forgot playing sick. Nazo's eyes closely followed her. She then said, "You are moving slower than I am." Niki heard this, and she started to walk faster.

Nazo kept talking, even when nobody was in front of her. However, from the kitchen, Ozra responded often with, "Really! No!" She acted as if she was hearing Nazo's every word.

Now Nazo wanted to learn about Ozra's household, and she asked, "What gifts did Shah Gul send your daughter last Eid?"

Niki was holding a cup of tea in one hand and a small dish full of *gur* in the other. She was about to enter the room when she heard Nazo's horrifying question.

"I heard that Baz Gul went to live with his Uzbek wife. Is that true?" Nazo, comfortably settled under the quilt of the *sandaly*, looked impatiently at the door for answers and her tea with *gur*.

Nazo stared at Niki as she entered the room. Even with her bad eyes, she noticed Niki's belly.

Many questions went through the old woman's mind, the main one being, *Is she pregnant? Is she pregnant?* Then she whispered to herself, "Like all other people, they probably cancelled the big wedding because of the war. I remember that they performed the *nikah* in order for Nur Gul to come and go freely. Still, she is not supposed to get pregnant while in her mother's house. It is an unforgivable sin. It will damage the Khan family honor."

She blamed herself because she was half deaf, and thought, *The illness of my old husband has made me stay in the house for so long that I no longer know what has gone on in the world.*

Niki placed the tea and *gur* in front of her, on top of the *sandaly*.

Nazo stayed silent, which made Niki worry. Nazo kept scratching her chin then said to herself, "I asked about the wedding, but I didn't hear what Ozra was saying."

She cursed herself again for being half-deaf and asking questions when Ozra was in the kitchen.

Soon, Ozra served lunch.

To keep Nazo quiet so as to not ask questions, Ozra filled her plate with lots of food. The old woman was hungry and focused her attention on eating, but her mind was on Niki, thinking that, *The girl is pregnant before her wedding. However, even it is shameful to get pregnant before going to the husband's house, Nur Gul and Niki had the* nikah.

That day, Nazo could not satisfy her curiosity whether Niki was pregnant, or had she grown fat? Being a rude woman, she could easily ask Niki if she was pregnant, but she feared Shah Gul's reaction if she asked the wrong question and knew that Niki would probably tell her mother-in-law.

After she finished eating, Nazo left. She was confused and decided soon to go visit Shah Gul, to get more information, and to satisfy her curiosity.

Ozra was hoping that Nazo—with all her sneezing, coughing, and coming from a long distance, as well as being so old—would not notice Niki's belly. Niki had been wearing a large dress with a shawl.

Did she notice Niki's belly? Ozra wondered. But she did not have the courage to bear the answer and bit her lips in shame.

Ozra told Niki, "This is not our way—to sleep with the fiancé before the wedding. What were you going to offer your husband on your wedding night? What would Shah Gul's reaction be? For some girls who became pregnant before the wedding, the child would still be seen as a bastard. What should I do? "

The night, when Ozra had noticed that her daughter was pregnant, was bitter cold, and she could not sleep. She went outside and squatted on the porch, feeling tired and breathless.

Even with the bitter cold, it was a beautiful snowy night. At any other time, Ozra loved to watch the falling snow. The little house of the old relatives on the side of the courtyard seemed like a small glass house when it snowed, but now it looked gloomy and isolated. She returned to the room and sat under the quilt of the *sandaly* next to Niki who was sleeping.

She remembered scandalous stories about girls who had destroyed their families' honor.

Some of them were lucky to get away. For the unfortunate ones, it was a scandal and became gossip for the village to tell for many years. If such a girl survived, she would have a low position in the eyes of her husband and his family; or she would remain in her parents' house with a bleak and uncertain future. Nobody would ever marry her, and she would grow old in her parents' house. Rarely, however, she might be killed by a family member.

"But nobody will kill my daughter because she was not raped nor did she have a love affair. I am sure that the child belongs to Nur Gul. By becoming pregnant before the wedding, she only will lose the big wedding and will live with embarrassment. Fortunately, we performed the *nikah*," Ozra comforted herself.

Ozra tried to go to sleep, but the memories of girls with such stories kept her awake. She remembered Safora.

Safora

Safora gave birth in her parents' home, out of wedlock. The child, a son, was stillborn. The mother of the young woman gave the now lifeless baby to their faithful servant along with some money, to bury in the graveyard, away from the village. The servant was supposed to have taken care of this.

That trusted servant, who had worked for the family for many years, did not take the body to the graveyard. Instead, she threw the little body into a stream flowing through their village.

Later, a farmer working on his irrigation ditch discovered the stillborn's body, stuck behind a grill. He picked up the tiny body, covered it with his *sadar,* a large piece of cloth that Afghan men wear over their shoulders, and carried it to the mosque. The village men in the mosque asked the *khadem*, a person who worked there, to bury the baby's remains in a corner of their village graveyard. They all believed that the body had flowed from the waters of another village.

The unfaithful servant took advantage of the family secret and began blackmailing Safora's mother. The blackmailing continued until the women of the house became annoyed and let the servant go. After leaving their house, she told the village people all about the mother of the dead baby found in the ditch.

The news echoed throughout the village and it became a big scandal. "The daughter of so and so gave birth to a bastard! And the father and brothers are walking the streets without shame!"

Safora's father and brothers, embarrassed that people were looking down on them, had a meeting and decided to get rid of Safora to restore their family's honor.

On the day they wanted to carry out their plan, the father sent the youngest son to lock the entrance gate. At the gate, the young boy who was close to his sister, paused, remembering all the good days he had with her. At that time, he wanted to run to his relatives in the alley and ask for help. He thought about his father and his brothers talking about the high importance of the family's honor. He changed his mind, put the latch on the gate, and walked to the house.

The mother asked Safora to take a bath and pray. Safora did not know what was going on, or why she needed to take a bath and pray—it was not the time for prayer.

In the other room, the father took his old rifle, cleaned it, and put one bullet in it. One single shot would end the embarrassment.

They entered Safora's bedroom, lined up in front of the surprised and very frightened girl, who saw the rifle in her father's hand. The father looked at each of his sons. It seemed that the decision was firm, except that he saw a different look in his youngest son's eyes.

Safora's mother decided that when the time came, she would go and drop herself at her husband's feet and beg for forgiveness. He would either accept his wife's plea or would kill her too for taking her daughter's side.

Earlier, Safora, while reciting her prayers, thought her father and brothers might marry her to one of her father's peasants as her punishment. She was deeply shocked when she saw her father with a rifle and her brothers beside him.

The father looked at his daughter's face and immediately turned his rifle away. He took out the single bullet, put it in his pocket, and threw the rifle to the floor. He ran to his daughter, hugged the frightened girl, and both started to cry. It was a rare and strange sight for an Afghan man to cry in front of his sons, wife, and daughter.

"I am not able to kill my own child. She has been so kind to me, and she deserves forgiveness. She is a female, and we were told that a female brain is less than a male's. I forgive her. Should I kill her because of people's talk?" the father said.

The brothers, who were excited earlier about saving their honor, had supported their father's intent to kill their sister. Being impressed by their father's tender emotion, they looked at their sister and agreed with their father's mercy.

The youngest brother knew how much his sister loved him and how she had helped his mother to raise him. He ran to his sister, hugged her, and said, "Our father is a kind man."

The mother prayed, thanking Allah for saving her daughter. But now she had a job—to find out who took the girl's honor away.

Soon the mother had the answer. Safora confessed about her love for the father of her baby. Her family would never approve of him because of an ages-old feud between the two families.

However, the boy and the girl still met each other in secret. The boy had told his mother about his great love for Safora and kept begging her to arrange his marriage to Safora, but because of the feud, she would never give her consent. Finally, the boy became frustrated and left the village, not knowing Safora was pregnant.

The elders of the family mediated between both families, and they agreed to let them marry. The boy returned, and the two became engaged.

Unfortunately, the girl, who felt immense fear and insult, grieved hard. She became sick and died before the wedding. The village girls made up songs about Safora's love story.

Remembering Safora's story and its tragic ending, Ozra began to weep hard. Then other stories of pregnant girls came to her mind—one after another. Remembering all these stories, she had a sleepless night.

Mahro

Mahro lived with her parents and brother in an old neighborhood in Kabul. Her father was the elder advocate of their alley. He was very protective of his only daughter and did not let her out of the house, or even go to school. She was only allowed to attend weddings of relatives.

She was a city girl but never walked in the city like the other girls. She had two favorite pastimes. One was listening to the radio. She knew the time of different programs on the Kabul radio, the names of most Afghani singers, and she loved to listen to the short dramas.

Her other favorite pastime was going to the rooftop. From the time her father and brother went to work, and until they returned late in the evening, she went there many times. The flat rooftop had high walls, up to her face. From the roof, she looked for hours at the city, watching from one corner to the other, waiting to talk with the neighbor girls when they came home from school, and watching the boys of the alley coming and going.

Her relatives' and neighbors' daughters often came to visit her. They talked to her about the outside world. Mahro wished that, like the other girls, she could go to school, to the public baths, to the shops, and to the movies. She wished she could ride the public bus.

Some of the girls envied her because most of the boys of their alley were in love with her radiant face. From her rooftop, she had affairs with several of them.

Mahro had a round face, fair skin, a nice straight nose, big brown eyes, and long brown hair. Most of the time, she wore her hair pulled into a thick single braid or ponytail. With her beautiful appearance, she won the hearts of the neighborhood boys.

She changed boyfriends often. She occasionally even managed to invite the favorite ones to come to meet her on the rooftop, where a small storage shed was located. It was her secret place to meet these boys. Her house backed up to a mountain slope, which made climbing to the roof easy for those lucky boys who got her invitation.

There was a rumor spreading among the neighbors that she had given birth and that her mother, early one morning, had taken the newborn baby to a wealthy man's house and left the baby on his doorstep. The man, after returning from morning prayer, saw the baby and took the baby inside.

Finally, Mahro married one of her boyfriends—the richest and the most naive one—who was madly in love with her. There was a big wedding for her. A car decorated with flowers, escorted by many relatives' cars from both families, took her to the groom's house.

"What happened after the wedding, when her mother-in-law came to check on the bloody handkerchief, the sign of her virginity?" curious girls and women were asking each other.

It was the tradition that, on the morning after the wedding, the mother-in-law or a female relative would go to the bride's room to check on the bride's virginity. On the bed, the mother-in-law would have placed a large handkerchief and then, with that same handkerchief, the bride was to clean up the virginal blood.

They said that Mahro's mother, on the night of the wedding, poured some pigeon's blood into a small jar, gave it to her daughter, and said, "When your husband goes to sleep, pour all the blood on the handkerchief, and in the morning let your mother-in-law see the bloody handkerchief."

Nobody really knew whether those rumors were true or not. When her mother-in-law heard these rumors, she accused the women and girls of being jealous of her beauty, good husband, and comfortable life.

The mother-in-law emphasized, "For me, honor comes first. If she were not a virgin, then I could have shaved her head, put her on a donkey, and sent her back to her mother's house—or I could have asked my husband to kill her. Now, I have the honor of telling people that I saw her virginity blood with my own eyes."

Thinking about those stories, Ozra lost much sleep during that long winter night. Outside, a strong wind started to blow, and she did not like the sound of the wind mixed with the barking dogs in the alley. The heat of the charcoal under the *sandaly* had faded.

Shivering with cold, she looked at her daughter's face. Niki was peacefully asleep next to her.

Pulling up the quilt and covering Niki's arms, Ozra said, "Sleep is a gift from Allah and soon one forgets the pain and misery."

Gold *Chamkaly*

Under the feeble light of the kerosene lamp, Ozra looked at her daughter's face, which shone like a beautiful porcelain doll, with arched eyebrows, long eyelashes, a straight little upward-turned nose, a well-formed mouth, and long hair the color of dates.

Ozra remembered that her mother had always talked about the legendary beauty of her grandmother. People even said that since Ozra and her mother did not inherit her beauty, then the great-granddaughter would inherit it.

"This is so true. Niki had indeed inherited her great-grandmother's legendary beauty," Ozra said to herself.

She visualized Niki as a beautiful bride, with all the women and girls of the village gasping at the fortunate bride of Nur Gul, son of the Khan, in her wedding gown wearing her mother-in-law's legendary gold *chamkaly* around her neck.

"Will I be that fortunate, as well, to see my daughter in a wedding gown and the gold *chamkaly* which Shah Gul promised her at the engagement party?" Ozra asked herself. The quilt resting on top of Niki's belly, higher on her body than usual, brought her back to the sad reality.

Ozra worried about Shah Gul's reaction and her daughter's fate while waiting for Nur Gul to come home.

She said, "There has been a mutual trust between Nur Gul and Niki—probably because they had grown up together." Thinking about Nur Gul gave Ozra strength.

He is like my relatives in Kabul, she thought, but soon remembered, "Even in Kabul, where the elite people in Afghanistan live, most families do not show mercy to their girls if they get pregnant in their parents' house—like Sohila, daughter of a prominent man in Kabul."

Sohila

Ozra remembered going with her relatives in Kabul to the funeral of Sohila, daughter of their old friend. Sohila had committed suicide. Ozra had known her and admired her beauty and her manners. She had been tall, with fair skin, long blonde hair, and blue eyes. Her family was from a province in the north of Afghanistan, where most people had those characteristics.

When they returned from the funeral, they spoke of the women there who were whispering that Sohila did not commit suicide. They said her father killed her after he learned that she had an affair with her Hazara classmate at Kabul University and that she was pregnant.

The Hazaras are a minority group in Afghanistan. They inhabit the northeast part of the country, and they are hard workers who went to Kabul to do the hardest work. In the past, they were rarely, if ever, accepted to the universities or military.

To keep his honor safe, Sohila's father, one of the elites of Kabul, told people that his daughter suffered from a mental problem and had committed suicide. Even being mentally ill or committing suicide in Afghanistan, as Ozra knew, was sinful and an embarrassment to the family's honor; but not as much as when a daughter becomes pregnant before marriage.

Ozra started to shiver nervously, seeing that her daughter, sleeping next to her, was pregnant and Nazo had come to visit them. Many questions came to her mind. *Had Nazo learned about Niki being pregnant? Who will Nazo tell, first? When will Nazo go to visit Shah Gul?* Then she calmed herself by thinking, *Why should I worry? My daughter and Nur Gul had already performed the* nikah. *She will lose only the big wedding*. Again, she felt comfort remembering that, because of the war, people had been canceling their weddings anyways. Ozra's thoughts were interrupted by bombardment blasting in the sky above Kabul, not far from their village. It was the time when the war was intensifying between the Communist government and the *Mujahedeen*.

Shocking News

The sounds of war increased every day. The explosion of bombs and echoes of gunfire were unrelenting. The country was being devastated by the Soviet occupiers; the new government's agents descended upon the villages searching and then looting homes for valuables and money, as well as taking many men to jail or prison. The Khans, Beys, landowners, and others who held positions in the previous government were the primary targets and were routinely rounded up to face unknown futures.

One day, Hajji Khan, Nur Gul's father, did not come home. His younger son, Zalmai, and some other relatives, including their next-door neighbor, Yaqub Khan, also a relative, started to search for him. After a few weeks, they were told that he was being held in the notorious prison of Pul-e-Charki.

Nazo, to satisfy her curiosity, went to visit Shah Gul. The two women sat and had tea. Nazo sipped the hot tea, being careful not to burn her toothless mouth. Shah Gul could tell that the surprise guest had something to say.

Shah Gul was having difficult days—her husband, Hajji Khan, was in the prison; Nur Gul had left for India; and she was fearful about Zalmai's safety. She was not ready for any further bad news.

Nazo finally said, "Sister, yesterday I went to see Ozra, and I saw Niki. Her belly was big . . . when is the baby due? Did you cancel the big wedding because of the war? These days, nobody tells me anything."

Hearing what Nazo just said, Shah Gul felt that something was not right. Shah Gul remembered that twice—recently—when she had gone to visit, Niki was sick, lying under the quilt of the *sandaly.*

Shah Gul was quick to respond and began to cry, saying, "At this moment, I do not care about other things. My husband is in prison . . . pray for me. You came at a time when I was on my way to the prison, taking my husband food and clothes."

Shah Gul got up quickly and, standing next to the door, called with a loud bossy voice for Sabro, her household servant.

Nazo did not dare ask any more questions.

Sabro rushed in, looking down at the floor.

Shah Gul told her, "Go tell the driver to get ready. Run, run, faster, idiot woman."

Then she told Nazo, "Come tomorrow. I will send you with Sabro to *ziart* (shrine) to help distribute *halwa* (sweets) for the poor. I will give you some money for your help. Now finish your tea, I have to get ready." Shah Gul turned and then walked quickly to her room.

Once in her room, Shah Gul sat on the floor, having a panic attack. She kept hitting her head with both hands, saying, "I hope this old blind woman is wrong." Then she lay on the floor and stayed there until she regained her peace of mind.

Nazo, while waiting for Shah Gul, eagerly filled her cup with tea, using several spoons of white sugar, and put large pieces of cookies in her mouth. She was happy that nobody was around to see her eating so greedily. She so much loved the rich people's tea with white sugar and cookies that she forgot all her other questions.

Shah Gul returned to the room. Nazo got up, said good-bye, and left. She was happy to come back tomorrow to go to *ziart* with Sabro, eat *halwa*, and receive some more money.

Without wasting time, Shah Gul and Sabro went to Sheen Klay Village to see Ozra and Niki. She decided not to make a big scene when she arrived. She greeted Ozra coldly and kindly asked Niki to get ready to go home with her. Ozra almost had a heart attack, seeing Shah Gul. However, she helped Niki pack her things and even put some cookies in her trunk. Niki was quiet, and her face had lost color. She was filled with fear.

Shah Gul then announced, "Because of the war, I cancelled the big wedding. I am glad that they did the *nikah*. Now, Niki reached the age to be in our house. Nur Gul will return in two months, and then during a small party, we will celebrate them becoming officially husband and wife."

Ozra walked them to the carriage with sad and worried eyes. She watched the carriage drive away until it disappeared at the end of the alley.

As soon as they came home, Shah Gul sent Sabro out and harshly told Niki, "My son has been gone for twelve months now. This is not his child." Then she screamed, "You are a whore! What should I do with you, and what should I tell people? Now, get lost from my face."

Niki immediately left the room. She hurriedly went down a hallway where she saw a door at the end. She opened the door and entered the room dragging her trunk behind her. That room was the *tawakhana*, a winter room next to the kitchen.

She was terrified, tired, and hungry. Remembering the cookies that her mother had packed, she ate some of them, wishing for a glass of water, milk, or tea—which was not around. She made a bed on the floor and soon went to sleep.

Early in the morning, the loud, harsh voice of her mother-in-law woke her up.

"You are sleeping in *tawakhana*? I forgot to tell you that your place is in the kitchen!"

To pay respect and greet her mother-in-law, she stood up and with a shaky voice, said, "*Salaam*."

"Do not say *salaam* to me. *Kanchani*!" Shah Gul said.

Kanchani referred to the notorious Indian dancers, who had lower positions in society, and was a common word used when people cursed girls or women who did wrong, Niki remembered.

Shah Gul's voice became horrified, "I am waiting for Nur Gul to come and see your belly with his own eyes and then, I will kill you." Shah Gul, with a furious voice, continued, "I have heard stories about honor killings, but I did not expect that it would happen in my own house."

Honor killing! She will kill me! Niki thought while her whole body trembled.

"Now, your job is to work in the stable. Feed the animals, keep the stalls clean, and collect the animals' dung for fuel," Shah Gul told her.

Niki did not mind working in the stable since she loved taking care of the animals. Two months had passed since Niki came to live with Shah Gul, but it seemed like a very, very long time.

Nur Gul completed his studies and returned home. On his first day back, his mother and brother told him about his father. Later, the mother, in private, told him about Niki.

Nur Gul kept quiet in front of his mother, believing that something bad had happened to Niki, his trusted and beloved fiancée.

He left his mother's room and went to see Niki.

Seeing Nur Gul at the kitchen door horrified Niki, but his peaceful face gave her strength, even as it made her feel confused.

Niki earnestly and truthfully told him what had happened to her and said, "Now, it is up to you to kill me, or . . . I do not know what to say. Whether you kill me or not, I beg you to not mention Baz Gul, my stepfather's name to anybody, because my mother will die if she learns what he did to me. My mother strongly believes that you came to visit me, and this for sure is your child." She stared at him for a response.

Nur Gul did not answer her, but he became furious and vowed to find Baz Gul and get revenge. He believed that Niki was fully innocent. He was, however, worried about how to convince his mother, while saving Niki, and keeping the family's honor intact.

Nur Gul's presence gave Niki immense peace.

He went to see his mother with a made-up story. "Mother, earlier I was too embarrassed to tell you that eight months ago, I came in privately to Afghanistan to pick up some documents. When I came, nobody was home. I then went to Sheen Klay and spent the night at Niki's house."

What Nur Gul said did not convince his mother. Shah Gul kept quiet. She did not want to make her already-worried son more worried.

A few days later, Yaqub Khan came to Nur Gul's house and told him that he had found someone who wanted a big bribe to release his father from the prison.

Nur Gul said, "I wish Zalmai had called me about my father. I would have left my studies and come home."

Yaqub Khan said, "Nobody knows for how long before they let a person free—one day, one week, or never—but we are lucky that Hajji Khan is alive." Yaqub Khan asked, "How come you did not come for a break?"

"To complete the program in fourteen months, we signed an agreement to study without a break," Nur Gul said. He immediately remembered his mother's presence in the room, and glanced at her. She made herself busy with her rosary, but she had already heard what he said.

Such a stupid boy. He should tell him that he came for a break eight months ago and stick to his lie. Otherwise, people will question where the child came from. She remembered an old expression, "Liars do not have good memories."

Soon, Nur Gul corrected himself, which gave his mother peace of mind that her son was not stupid.

He said, "I came to Kabul eight months ago, for only a short visit, to get some documents. I stopped at our house. My mother and Zalmai were not home, so I went to Aunt Ozra, and she did not tell me about my father, thinking I knew. She did not want to disturb me anymore."

Yaqub Khan said, "I am glad you are home now. Have the money ready for the bribe."

Shah Gul had money to pay the large bribe, and Hajji Khan was released from prison. Shah Gul, on seeing her husband released from the horrible prison, gave food for the poor.

Hajji Khan was happy to be home. He thanked Allah for Nur Gul being back home and that his daughter-in-law was pregnant. He naturally thought that, since Niki was home, Shah Gul had probably brought Niki into the house with a small ceremony. He wished for a grandson.

Shah Gul did not share Niki's situation with her husband, waiting for the right time to handle it. She did not want anything to hurt their honor. To not make her husband suspicious, she let the girl sleep in *tawakhana* with Nur Gul.

At the mosque, Hajji Khan spoke about his terrible experience in the notorious *Pul-e-charki* prison, which horrified his audience. Most of the men in his village vowed to leave Afghanistan and join the *Mujahedeen* in Pakistan. At the time, Pakistan, for political reasons, welcomed all Afghan refugees and allowed the *Mujahedeen* to organize against the Afghan Communist government, from their soil.

The worsening war situation compelled both Nur Gul and Yaqub Khan to start preparing their families' departures from their beloved homeland.

Chapter 4

Niki was now in the last days of her pregnancy. One day, she was not feeling well, with pain coming and going throughout the day. She endured the pain and finished her chores. On many evenings, she put on her thick shawl and went to the rooftop, where she would think about her life.

This night, she sat in her usual corner. It was a cold spring night in April. A full moon was shining in the far corner of the sky, moving slowly toward the village. In the moonlight, the villagers' little houses looked like images in black-and-white pictures.

She gazed at the lapis-lazuli clear sky with its twinkling golden stars. She was hoping to see a shooting star, to make a wish. She had heard from Roya, her relative and friend in Kabul, that when a person sees a shooting star, that person should then make a wish.

From the rooftop, she saw Nur Gul with his father and brother leaving the house, going to the mosque for prayer.

She felt her baby move, followed by a sharp pain in her belly. Fear and anxiety increased her pain. She managed to walk downstairs and went to her mother-in-law's room. "I have pain!" She cried out, as she held onto the doorframe.

The mother-in-law got up, walked toward her, and said in a gentle tone, "I was waiting for this moment, to make you a goose-feather bed, to prepare warm water with perfumed soap, colorful towels, and to fix *liti*, that sweet food for after the birth! I am sending someone for the midwife, plus I will send Sabro's son to bring your dear mother to see you giving birth also . . ."

For a moment, Niki visualized a fantasy world, and remembered seeing goose-feather quilts at Roya's house in Kabul, scented soaps which Nur Gul always brought her in pink and light green colors which had a pleasant aroma, and the *liti!*

Her fantasy did not last long when she heard, "A *harami* is going to be born in my house!"

Then she felt hard smacks on her head, making her dizzy. Her mother-in-law grabbed her hair with one hand and with the other started to hit her on the head, face, eyes, shoulders, back, and chest. Then she dragged the surprised girl out of the house all the way to the stable, on the other side of the courtyard.

"You think that you can give birth to a *harami* under my roof? No, you are going to give birth in the stable! By tomorrow, you will die, and I will tell people that you became sick and died! Our honor will be saved," the mother-in-law said with her harsh voice. She continued cursing, saying, "We are fortunate that we performed the *nikah* and because of the war, like other people who called off their children's big weddings, people will think that we cancelled the wedding too and brought you home. No one will become suspicious. But you have to tell me the truth—who your lover is, and why you chose him over Nur Gul?"

Niki could not tell her mother-in-law that she was raped by Baz Gul. She told herself, *The truth would have killed my mother. Since I love her so much, I can endure all the suffering and keep the secret with me. But I vowed to tell the truth to Nur Gul, which I did. He knows that nobody in the world will take his place in my heart*. She then closed her eyes and let Shah Gul continue beating her. That moment, she was not thinking about herself. She was thinking about the two people that she loved more than her own life.

Shah Gul's blows on Niki's eyes and ears were the most painful ones. Her hands were so heavy it felt like she was holding rocks in them. When they reached the stable door, Shah Gul looked around and saw wooden stakes on the ground. She picked up one of them and began striking Niki harder and harder with it until Niki fell to the ground. Her shawl had fallen off, her dress was all torn apart, and her once-braided hair was now mostly undone.

Then Shah Gul opened the stable door, pulled Niki by her hair, and pushed her in. She slammed the door, put the latch on, and turned away. She saw Niki's shawl on the ground, picked it up, opened the stable door again, threw the shawl inside, and ran like a crazy person toward the house. Near the porch, she missed a step, fell, and broke her leg. She crawled to the house in much pain, cursing Niki and hoping she would die in the stable.

When Niki was pushed in, the stable seemed totally dark. She felt blood rush to her face and felt like she was dying. Her body became numb from all the beatings, and she felt deeply humiliated. She had no answer as to why all these things were happening to her.

Soon her eyes, in the now half-dark stable, were able to see. Faint moonlight was coming from a round hole in the wall close to the ceiling. She had no fear of being in the stable because most of her chores were to work there and feed the animals. She milked the cow and goat and collected animal dung for fuel. She was not a stranger to the yellow cow, the two strong gray oxen with white foreheads, the white horse, the two goats, and the donkey.

That night, her entrance into the stable was quite unlike the other times. The animals sensed something unusual and turned their heads toward the stable door.

Niki felt that the ox's look was fatherly, as if he was asking her, "What is wrong?" The white horse in the far corner offered her comfort with a faithful look. The goats stopped playing with each other, sitting across from her and staring curiously at her. The donkey looked confused, as though trying to figure out what was exactly happening.

The large eyes of the yellow cow looked at Niki with kindness, which gave Niki courage to drag her weakened and broken body over to sit next to her. Having been severely beaten, she found solace in talking to the animals. "I am your guest tonight," she told them. Looking at the donkey, she thought, *The donkey will never figure out what is going on.* Although she was consumed with unending pain, that thought made her smile.

Her contractions soon began coming closer and closer together. They brought tears to her eyes, and she wondered what would happen next. It was then that someone opened the stable door and entered. Niki thought that her mother-in-law had come back. She shivered, wondering if she would soon be killed.

"It is me, Amira. Let's go to my house before the men return from the mosque. Later, I will bring you back home and make your mother-in-law be at peace with you," Amira said.

Yaqub Khan's wife, Amira, the next-door neighbor, had been on their rooftop and had seen the dragging scene; but she had not heard what Shah Gul was saying. She had never seen Shah Gul that angry.

She did not immediately get involved. But after she saw Shah Gul put Niki in the stable, she decided she needed to and would also mediate between them. Without wasting any more time, she hurried to the stable.

"Aunt, I am in labor," Niki faintly said.

"You are in labor?" Amira worriedly asked. "Probably Shah Gul did not know that you were in labor when she put you in the stable. Let me go and tell her," Amira said.

"No, no, I beg you, I beg you. She put me here to die by tomorrow because I became pregnant in my mother's house. Please help me," she said faintly.

"For now, then, let's go to my house," Amira said, and she helped Niki walk. They were about to leave, when from a hole in the gate, Amira peeped outside and saw, from far away, the men returning from the mosque. Their shadows in the moonlight were like tall giants walking in slow motion. The women remained in the stable, which was half lit by that same moonlight.

Niki cried out, "Aunt, the baby . . . my pain is too strong . . ."

"Lie down, my daughter," Amira said, placing her hand on Niki's belly, which now seemed so big. She helped her lie in the right position to give birth.

Niki stuffed a corner of her shawl into her mouth to suffocate her loud cries.

Soon, a girl was born.

"Praise to Allah! You gave birth so easily," Amira whispered and covered the newborn with her large veil while waiting for the placenta to emerge.

Suddenly Niki pulled Amira's hand toward her belly and moaned again in sharp pain. Another birth was coming, and another girl. At birth, each baby made a loud cry. Amira placed the second baby next to the first one and covered both with her large veil.

Now, completely exhausted, Niki fainted. This worried Amira. She ran to the animals' water tank, wetted part of Niki's shawl, and put it on Niki's forehead, shaking her shoulders saying, "My daughter, keep yourself awake." Amira's heart was beating fast, and she was thinking that any minute, the men would enter the gate. Soon they did, and walked the long courtyard toward the house. Amira held her breath while the men were passing the stable. The sound of steps vanished, and Amira let her breath out.

"Let's get out of here," she said.

She helped Niki get up and held both babies for her. They started to walk. Niki opened the gate carefully. It was old and made a creaking sound if somebody opened or closed it carelessly.

They left the stable and walked in the alley to the next door. For Niki, it seemed too far to go. She remembered this same feeling once before, the day when Baz Gul raped her and she had to walk down a similar alley to Shinky's house.

She had the same dreadful feeling this night. Now, she had even more pain. She kept dragging herself along, following Amira. Fortunately, no one was in the alley.

Amira, holding the babies, felt uncomfortable to be walking outside the house without her veil, which she used to cover the babies. She hoped that nobody would show up in the alley and focused on her gate, trying to reach it as soon as possible. Niki could only move very slowly.

They were about to enter Amira's house when Niki suddenly fell to the ground. Amira, while still holding the two babies, opened the gate with her foot. Amira's daughter, Robia, and her husband, Yaqub Khan, were in the courtyard. She told them to help Niki, who was lying on the ground outside.

Yaqub Khan looked at his wife, without her veil, and saw her holding something. He nonetheless rushed outside, picked up the young woman from the ground, and brought her into the house.

Yaqub Khan, who had a humble nature, was angry at his wife for being without a veil and for getting involved with other people's business; but when he saw Niki's condition, he could only ask, "What happened to her? A wild animal attack her?"

"I will tell you what happened," Amira said, while asking Robia to run to the kitchen and fix a glass of lemonade and sugar for Niki.

After putting Niki and her babies in the guest room, Robia went to the kitchen to fix the lemonade. She mixed sugar in the water, added some lemon drops, and brought it to the young woman who—again—had fainted.

Amira ran to get a wet towel to place on Niki's forehead. Then she poured drops of lemonade in her mouth.

Niki regained consciousness but stayed motionless in the bed. Amira gave her a small amount of opium to kill the pain and then covered her with a quilt. She then began to care for the newborns. Finally, she went to the kitchen to fix eggs and *liti* for the new mother to help her regain her strength. After feeding Niki, who was now starting to move, she helped her wash, handing her pink soap with a wonderful aroma.

Niki looked at Amira. She made sure that this time she was not imagining all the good things happening to her. "I can smell the aroma of the soap," she told herself.

Her wounded eyes were expressing millions of thanks and prayers. Weakly, she said, "Aunt, may Allah give you all the blessings."

The opium took effect, and Niki was about to go to sleep.

Amira told her, "This evening, I went to the roof to pick up something. I saw the scene when Shah Gul was dragging you. After she put you in the stable, I ran downstairs and told Robia what I had seen and made her wait for me. Then I came to the stable."

Robia interrupted her mother, saying, "I waited for a long time on the roof. I saw men slowly coming from the mosque. When they entered the alley, they stopped at each other's door for a few minutes to finish their conversations."

Niki surrendered to sleep, and Amira went to tell her husband what had happened that evening. Yaqub Khan listened to his wife and then thanked Allah for the life of the young mother and her babies.

"Go make them ready. I will take them to her mother's house." Then he called his son, Share Jan, to accompany them and make ready his horse for the carriage.

"May I call our car driver?" his son asked.

"No. I will take them by the carriage to take the short cut, and nobody should know that we are taking her to Sheen Klay Village. It is not very far. We will go drop them off and then return," he said while adding, "I will talk to Nur Gul tomorrow."

"She cannot hold two babies. I will go with you too," Amira said.

Amira hurriedly got her house guest and the two babies prepared for the trip. Share Jan helped his mother get in the carriage with the babies in the front, and then he helped Niki lie down in the back seat. He drove the carriage while his father rode his horse in front.

When they left the house, they saw Nur Gul quickly running out of the house. Yaqub Khan and his companions were surprised to see him.

When Nur Gul saw his neighbors, he stopped to greet them.

"My son, is everything going well with you?" Yaqub Khan asked.

"This evening, when we were in the mosque, my mother fell on the stairs and broke her leg. I am going to bring Gulam, the *shekestaband,* to put her broken bones in a cast."

"Son, what can I do for you?" Yaqub Khan offered his help.

"You are very kind," he said.

While Nur Gul was speaking to Yaqub Khan, he kept his distance because Yaqub Khan had women with him.

Niki whispered to Amira, "Aunt, tell him about me. He is on my side." Amira told Yaqub Khan what Niki said. He thought for a second and then agreed to tell Nur Gul.

Nur Gul had just started to walk away when Yaqub Khan called for him. "Son, wait! There is something urgent to tell you! After taking care of your mother, meet me in front of the old caravansary. Nobody can know about our meeting."

At the outskirt of Angur Dara, there was an old vacant caravansary, a kind of inn with a large central court where travelers with their caravans would stop for the night for rest and food.

"Son, it is very urgent!" Amira also added.

Nur Gul heard Amira's voice, turned around, and said, "Salaam Alikum, aunt. I will be there."

Nur Gul wondered what Yaqub Khan would tell him. He walked fast toward the *shekestaband*'s house, which was about five minutes away. When he reached the house, the *shekastaband*'s son opened the door, greeted the Khan's son, and said, "If you are looking for my father, he is not home!"

"Will he be home soon?" Nur Gul asked anxiously.

Then from the corner of the alley came the *shekestaband*'s voice. "I am back." Now Nur Gul would not be late for his meeting at the old caravansary.

Chapter 5

Yaqub Khan's small caravan took a zigzagging dirt path and headed toward the old caravansary on the outskirts of the village. The light from the full moon made the trip easy. The night's silence was disturbed only by the sound of a nearby farmer, in charge of irrigation, singing a folk song.

They passed the village's graveyard, and as the custom, they prayed for the dead. Women feared passing graveyards at night, especially the night of a full moon, when the tombs were visible. Shortly, they reached the old caravansary. The women with the babies came down from the carriage and sat on the porch of the old ranch-type building in ruins. The men stayed next to their horses and waited for Nur Gul.

Niki let Amira know that she was bleeding. Amira gave her a towel to use. She started to walk slowly and entered one of the old roofless rooms next to the porch to take care of her business. The moonlight helped her find her way.

On her way back to the porch, she felt weak and put her hand on the wall for support. Her fingers caught on a thin strip of cloth coming from a row of well-worn bricks which caused a brick to fall along with some other things.

She collected her strength and yelled, "Aunt, aunt, come here." Amira placed the babies on the ground and ran to see Niki.

"Aunt, a strip of cloth was hanging on the wall. It caught my fingers. I pulled it, a brick fell, and all these things from a hole behind the brick fell to the ground," she said while pointing to a small heap of colored stones and coins shining in the moonlight in the roofless back room.

Amira took one of the coins and said, excitedly, "It is gold! You stay here."

Soon Amira returned with her husband. He took a close look at the findings and then left.

He returned with a saddlebag, picked them all up from the ground, and put them in it. He poked his hand into the hole seeking any further treasure.

"Be careful, a scorpion or something else can hurt you from inside that old wall," Amira said.

"The weather is still cold, and everything is dead," he said and put his hand up to his elbow into the hole. He touched more pieces and took them out. Inside the wall was a broken clay vase. It was very old and was the vessel left with the treasure.

He picked up a few nearby worn mud bricks and sealed the hole.

Yaqub Khan said, "Probably in the past somebody hid this treasure in this wall. Nobody should know about what we found. People will loot us. But we will tell Nur Gul."

Then he turned to Niki and said, "Daughter, these are your treasures because you found them."

"Uncle, how could they be mine? You brought me here, and you saved my life," Niki said.

Share Jan, being a typical young boy, paid no attention to what was going on in the room next to the porch. He took advantage of the time, sat on his seat in the carriage, closed his eyes, and tried to sleep.

Niki followed Yaqub Khan and Amira back to the porch. From the porch, Niki looked down the road, which seemed so long, ending finally in a faraway dark point. Her pain increased. Amira had taken some opium with her when leaving the house. She gave a small piece to Niki to put under her tongue and help ease her pain.

While waiting, Amira remembered that her father often had talked about this caravansary. For centuries, caravans loaded with expensive goods had passed through the Afghan land, going back and forth to India and regions beyond the Amu River, Samarqand, and Bukhara.

The merchants, while staying in the caravansary, also brought with them stories to share with each other. Some stories were greatly exaggerated. Men, from the surrounding villages who worked there, listened to these stories and retold them to their families. The most famous story was about Princess Jahantab of Samarqand and Prince Slaimon of India.

To keep Niki's mind busy, Amira wanted to tell her that story. Before starting, she covered Niki with a blanket to keep her warm, and then she began:

"Once upon a time, there was an Indian merchant who used to go to Samarqand to sell embroidered silk fabrics to the ladies in the royal palace. On his last trip, the merchant saw Princess Jahantab of Samarqand, the most beautiful girl he had ever seen. He had heard stories of her legendary beauty.

"When the merchant returned, he brought merchandise from Samarqand to India's royal palace. He also spoke about the beauty of the Samarqand princess. The Indian prince, who happened to be nearby, heard the merchant. At the end of his business, he asked the merchant to take him to Samarqand to see this beautiful princess himself.

"They set off for Samarqand. When they reached Kabul to rest, they stopped next to the bank of the Kabul River. The river had a muddy, light-brown color, a sign of a recent flood. As the prince sat on the bank and thought about the unknown princess, he noticed something shiny, partially sticking from the mud. He dug in the muddy river bank and found a magnificent golden bracelet encrusted with colorful jewels. He picked it up, showed it to his companion, and put it in his pocket.

"In Samarqand, he disguised himself as a coworker of the merchant and entered the palace. He saw the beautiful princess. At first glance, he fell in love with her.

"Soon there was an announcement from the king of Samarqand that Princess Jahantab was ready to get married. There was to be a contest among the suitors, requiring each suitor to demonstrate that he was strong, brave, and could afford the highest bride price.

"Kings, princes, wealthy young and old men, and famous wrestlers from neighboring and faraway countries, who had heard about the contest and its prize of a beautiful princess, traveled to Samarqand to participate.

"The Indian merchant believed in his prince's physical ability, but he worried that the prince, who was not as wealthy as the other participants, could not pay a high bride price.

"Prince Slaimon won the physical contest. As for the bride price, he humbly presented the bracelet, which he had found on the bank of the Kabul River.

"Skillful jewelers of the region were invited to examine the jewels of the suitor. The Indian prince and his companion were surprised when they learned that the bracelet, which he presented, was worth seven times more than the entire Kingdom of Samarqand!

"The king of Samarqand married his daughter to Prince Slaimon of India and had a majestic and spectacular wedding for them. The groom took his bride to India and there they lived happily forever."

During the story, Niki was thinking of Nur Gul as Prince Slaimon and herself as Princess Jahantab. At the end of the story, Nur Gul appeared on the road, riding toward them.

Amira told Nur Gul what had happened to Niki. The young man was shocked at what he heard, and being grateful for his wife's survival, expressed his appreciations for all their help. In a hushed tone, he said, "Now you may go home. It is my responsibility to take Niki to Sheen Klay."

"Son, we have to be together. Your wife needs your aunt's help," Yaqub Khan said.

With those words of assistance, they all continued their trip.

Niki thought that in the company of nice people, the moonlight, the tall trees and the narrow streams on both sides of the road; and being with Nur Gul, the journey would be pleasant. *But no, I still have pain in my eyes, jaw, and head.* She closed her eyes. The uneven road made the carriage bounce constantly and rock from side to side. The opium fortunately was taking effect.

They were about to reach Sheen Klay, heading toward the main road, when they saw a car coming from the opposite side. When the car came closer, it stopped in front of them. A man rolled the window down and said, "Brothers, it is impossible to travel this way. At the end of the road, Afghan officers with Soviet soldiers are patrolling to catch young boys for compulsory military service and to rob the other passengers. They searched us and took our valuables. You better go back where you came from."

The man introduced himself. He was from a little village past Angur Dara. After a few further words, he said good-bye, rolled the window up, and drove off, leaving the air cloudy from the dust left behind.

Yaqub Khan accepted the kind man's warning and turned around his small caravan to go back home.

When they again were passing by the village's graveyard, Amira and Niki quietly recited some familiar verses from the Holy Qur'an. The women prayed and were immersed in deep spiritual thought. The men were thinking completely other thoughts when they abruptly heard a loud, deep voice, yelling, "Stop! Throw your valuables on the ground."

Niki was shaken from her prayers, and the suddenness of the encounter frightened her, as if ghosts had come out from the tombs. From behind a broken wall, around a few moonlit tombs, two men jumped out and slowly crept to them, holding knives.

Yaqub Khan noticed that they were not from their village. That part of the graveyard was the rendezvous place for the local hashish smokers. They usually asked for money or food, but they never robbed the night travelers from their own village.

With a voice full of authority, Yaqub Khan told them, "Brothers, we have women with us. Keep your distance. We will give you all our valuables."

One of them said, "Then one at a time, come, give me your valuables and money."

The travelers obeyed. The boss held the money and watches.

The other one commanded Yaqub Khan, "Throw me your saddlebag."

Yaqub Khan said, "The saddlebag is full of women's clothes. If you need women's clothes, then take them."

He detached the bag and threw it to the man.

The boss felt insulted, cursed this man, and yelled, "Don't touch women's clothes. You bastard, we're robbers, but we are not men without honor." The robber, who had just grabbed the bag, threw it back to Yaqub Khan and mumbled, "It felt heavy . . . like it had rocks in it."

The boss again ordered the male travelers to give up their possessions, "Throw your jackets, hats, shawls, and shoes on the ground. Then you are free to go."

Yaqub Khan and his male companions, Nur Gul and Share Jan, began to shiver in the cold night air after giving over their clothes.

While going home, Yaqub Khan recited a famous Persian poem of Saadi Shirazi, one of the major Persian poets of the medieval period, "*Een tcha shour ist ka dour-e-quamar mebinam and hama afaqh per az fetna wa shar mebinam.*" (It means: What kind of chaos I see around the moon, corruptions and disasters in the entire world.)

When they safely reached home, Yaqub Khan thanked Allah for their safety. Robia was surprised by their quick return.

Amira told her, "The road was occupied by soldiers."

She then asked Robia to watch the babies. The four huddled in the adjoining room to privately discuss Niki's future and what they had found.

"Niki will stay in our house like our own daughter, as long as you want her to," Amira said to Nur Gul, a new father with little choice in the matter. He greatly appreciated their help and hospitality and, without any hesitation, agreed.

Then Yaqub Khan told Nur Gul about the treasure that Niki found.

"I do not want to report this to the authorities. They will think that we had found more and had returned only a part of it. They will never believe us. Also, the time is not right. These communists kill people easily for a small amount of money. At this moment, I am not sure if the jewels are real. However, they belong to Niki."

After engaging in further discussion, they finally decided to split the findings. While Yaqub Khan and Amira were talking, Nur Gul glanced at his wife, and with the light from the gasoline lamp, he saw Niki's swollen face. The side of her mouth was cut, a thick line of blood had collected on her lips, and her eyes were swollen. With a breaking heart, he remained silent, embarrassed to say a word to her in the presence of his elders. Nur Gul thanked Allah for having such helpful and kind neighbors.

Yaqub Khan was proud of himself. He rubbed his mustache and said, "Such a night full of adventure! We are blessed that all of us are safe!" He emphasized, "Nobody should know that Niki is in our house, and no word spoken about what we have found. I did not even tell my own son."

Amira then asked, "What did you feel when you threw the saddlebag to the robbers?"

"I believe in destiny. If it is in our destiny to have it, then we will have it," Yaqub Khan said.

"We have to go see my best friend who owns Mirza's jewelry store in Pul-e-Bagh Oumoumi bazaar, across the Kabul River. I will take with me a few of these stones and coins for him to examine and appraise."

When Nur Gul was ready to leave, he asked, "What should I tell my mother about where Niki is?"

Niki remembered what Nur Gul had said earlier about his mother who broke her leg. She thought a moment and then answered, "Tell her that upon your returning from the mosque, you checked the stable, and you saw me there. You thought that I was still working in the stable and not feeling well. You were afraid I might give birth in the stable, so you took me to my mother's house."

Everyone agreed that this would be the best answer.

"Your daughters are as beautiful as their mother," Amira said, even though she knew it was not proper to compliment baby girls in front of an older man.

"Daughters?" Nur Gul asked in surprise.

"You have twin daughters!" she said. Amira believed that Nur Gul was too shy to go see the baby girls.

Nur Gul kissed Yaqub Khan and Amira's hands and said goodbye. He glanced at his wife and left quietly thinking, "In one single night, so many surprises!"

Niki and the babies stayed in the guest room which was furnished with an Afghani carpet, red velvet mattresses with matching satin cushions and a quilt.

"Such a night! From the stable to the guest room of a Khan!" Niki said to herself, still suffering from pain and fatigue. She wondered if her mother-in-law was satisfied in trying to kill her to save the family's honor. She finally fell asleep, as dawn approached.

Chapter 6

Shah Gul had a very eventful evening as well. She had locked Niki in the stable. Panting and walking in a hurry to get inside the house, hoping all the while that nobody saw her and what she had done, she missed a step on the porch. She fell and broke her leg. She swallowed hard and tried not to cry, and in much pain, she crawled into the house and then to her room. She crawled until she reached her trunk in the corner. She opened it, and from a clay jar, took out a small piece of opium to kill her pain.

The men of the house eventually returned from the mosque. As usual, they talked about the *mullah*'s preaching of that night: the forced recruitment of young boys to the military.

Then the father turned on his radio to listen to the BBC's Persian/Pashto news. After the Communist takeover in Afghanistan, listening to BBC News in the Afghan cities and villages became a rapidly growing phenomenon. People were showing their defiance by secretly listening to the broadcasts every evening.

The news concerned the same topic, which the *mullah* had preached: the central government controlled by the Soviet government was recruiting young boys, by force, to join its ranks. Boys who refused to join would be killed immediately or be sent to unknown places.

The father said, "During the time of Zahir Shah, it was mandatory for males, upon reaching their twenty-second birthday, to serve in the military for two years. But now it was very different. Now the military was forcefully recruiting boys of all ages and even the smallest children were not safe. The boys would be sent to the Soviet Union for military training."

Then the father looked around and asked his sons, "Where is your mother?"

Shah Gul usually joined them when they returned from the mosque. She would fix them some fruits or desserts to eat while they would converse.

Soon they heard moaning sounds from Shah Gul. The boys ran first, and their father quickly followed.

"I broke my leg. Send Nur Gul to bring the *shekestaband*, to fix my leg," she requested. She then asked Zalmai to go and get Sabro to come help also.

Nur Gul left in a hurry to get the *shekestaband*. It was there at the gate that he met his next-door neighbors who asked him to meet them at the old caravansary.

Nur Gul brought the *shekestaband* home to attend to his mother's leg.

That night, Sabro slept in Shah Gul's room, to offer help if needed. The father went to sleep in another room. With the help of the opium, Shah Gul soon fell asleep.

Nur Gul came out of the house, went to the stable to get his horse, and headed to the old caravansary.

After a few hours, Shah Gul woke up, thinking, *If my husband and my sons knew what I did, they might praise me. I am saving their honor!*

Suddenly a sense of remorse filled her heart. She visualized Niki in the stable where the air was stagnant and cold, with animals toppling all over her body. She had given birth to a baby under the hooves of the animals. Shah Gul, with great pain and a cast on her leg, slowly limped to the stable, to save Niki. Sabro, who was supposed to watch the injured woman, was fast asleep and did not hear Shah Gul staggering out of the room.

When Shah Gul reached the stable, she put her ear on the door and listened. She heard nothing. She muttered under her breath, "I killed Niki."

She frantically opened the stable door and cried out, "Niki, Niki." It seemed that the animals themselves were turning away from this cruel woman. She cried out again, "Niki, if you answer, I will give food for the poor, just respond to me." She kept saying to herself, "Repent, repent, repent."

At that moment, the yellow cow pushed his hoof against her broken leg which caused her horrible pain. It seemed the other animals wanted to hurt her too. The air of the stable made her ill. She started to choke and gasp for fresh air. She cried for help while trying to leave the stable and its stench, but nobody heard her. She didn't leave quick enough. A kick from the donkey dropped her to the floor, hitting her head against the stable door before falling to the ground. Soon her face and clothes were covered with animals' dung.

It was almost time for morning prayers when Nur Gul returned home from his long night full of adventures. He headed to the stable to put his horse back and found his mother there, lying unconscious beside the stable door where she had fallen.

"What a night! Things are still happening," he said and tried to pick up his mother. He found her too heavy to carry himself. He ran inside the house to wake up his brother Zalmai. They both went to the unconscious woman and, with great difficulty, carried her inside. They shook Sabro who was soundly asleep.

She woke up and awkwardly looked around and asked what was going on. The young men asked her to help with their mother. Sabro did as she was told. Shah Gul was cleaned and clothed, and then placed in bed. The mother was in a very deep sleep or was still unconscious.

Nur Gul said loudly, "Probably she took too much opium to kill her pain." Then he thought, *I am sure she went to check on Niki and fell again.*

Finally, the two brothers went to their rooms to get some sleep as well. On the way, Zalmai asked, "What is going on and where is my sister-in-law?"

"It's a long story. I'll tell you tomorrow," Nur Gul said and walked to his room. There, he thought about Niki's ordeal from the squalor of a stable to the guest room of a Khan. His thoughts were interrupted when his father called out, "Let's go to the mosque for morning prayer."

Chapter 7

It was noon when Niki woke up. For a moment, she was not able to recognize her surroundings. The ceiling was made of nicely painted long beams, the walls were white, and a colorful curtain covered the large window. The sun was shining directly through the transparent fabric showing the outlines of colorful flowers.

"Did I have a nightmare followed by this pleasant dream? My mother-in-law beat me, locked me in the stable, causing me much pain . . ." In a haze, she looked around. Soon, she recognized that this was in the guest room of Aunt Amira.

She was relieved to see her babies asleep quietly in the corner. She dragged herself to them. She stared at them and gently caressed their heads and faces. She noticed prayer charms around their necks. She bent to kiss the verses of the Holy Qur'an carved on them.

Amira entered the room holding a tray of food—a few raw eggs, milk, and *liti*, and a teapot of black tea with brown sugar, crushed walnuts, and ginger, a typical village hot drink recipe for a woman who has recently given birth.

"*Salaam Alikum*, aunt!" Niki said, as she tried to stand up to greet her.

"Do not get up, my daughter," Amira said and bent herself to kiss her wounded forehead. She then recited a few verses from the Holy Qur'an and thanked Allah for all His blessings.

"We have already taken care of the babies. And I gave them the prayer charms of my daughters, Amina and Robia. They wore those charms around their necks for many years," Amira told her gently, "Now it is time for your daughters to do the same."

"Aunt, I wish you all the blessings in the world for the good things you are doing for me," Niki said and then thought, *If she knew that the twins were* haramis, *and the product of a rape, would she still treat me this good?"*

"What are you thinking about with that sorrowful look on your face? Be grateful for all the blessings. The mother-in-law and daughter-in-law fight is not something new. When the time is right, I will mediate between the two of you. Now, eat your food," Amira said.

Niki thought, *I wish it was as simple as you think.* She smiled at Aunt Amira and turned to her food. Even though she was hungry, she still did not like eating raw eggs, although they were good for new mothers. She covered her nose and poured all of it, quickly, into her mouth, thinking about *liti,* her favorite sweet.

But things soon changed for the worse. Later that day, Niki became very ill with a high fever.

"We have to take her to the hospital," Amira said and sent her son to call Nur Gul.

When Nur Gul came, he agreed that Niki needed to go to the hospital and wanted to take her there himself. Yaqub Khan sent for his driver.

"Son, your Aunt Amira and I will take Niki to the hospital, to avoid questions, if somebody sees us, they will think it's Robia," Yaqub Khan said.

On the way, Niki moaned, her injuries causing her constant and unrelenting pain. The driver heard her and began speeding faster to the hospital.

Amira held her gently and said, "Dear daughter, you will be fine. We are about to reach the hospital." The hospital was about one hour away.

At the Wazir Akbar Khan Hospital, the doctor on duty, after learning that the patient had given birth last night, recommended taking her to the Malalai Women's Hospital. Niki felt that her pain would never end. This hospital was ten miles further.

At Malalai Women's Hospital, a young female doctor on duty examined her, and then spoke with Amira. "It seems that she gave birth with no problem. But she is suffering from injuries all over her body. Did someone beat her violently? Did she give birth to a girl?"

"Twin girls," Amira said.

"It is no surprise that she was beaten, just like many other women who give birth to girls are beaten by their husbands or their husbands' family members. I hope that her kidneys, lungs, and other organs were not damaged. I am going to call the police!" the doctor said with a firm voice.

"Please don't do it. I beg you. If you call the police, the situation will get worse. Her husband's family will punish us because we are helping this young woman and her future will be in danger. Please trust me. I will take care of everything," Amira humbly said.

The young female doctor left the room and soon returned with her supervisor, a male doctor. He agreed with the duty doctor that the patient had given birth with no complications. They prescribed some medications. Both doctors advised Amira to take Niki to another hospital, as soon as possible, to treat her injuries.

They took her back to the first hospital. A male doctor began treating her and said, "She is lucky to be alive with this deeply cut scalp. I have to use many stitches to bring the wound together and give her medications to bring down the fever. If her pain does not stop, or the fever does not go away in a day or so, bring her back here immediately," he said.

The doctor then became upset. "Who hit her so hard and why? I am going to report this to the police. This beating of women must stop."

Amira begged this doctor, too, not to report this matter to the police. She did not want anyone from Nur Gul's family to know she was helping Niki.

On the way home, they stopped at a pharmacy. Yaqub Khan went inside, bought the medication, and returned to the car. Amira said she also needed to buy things for the mother and the twin babies. She walked to the pharmacy and also to the shops next to it. After she bought the necessary items, they headed home.

For the next few days, Niki was bedbound, recuperating. Amira and Robia took care of her and the infant twins.

***

Meanwhile, at the mosque, Hajji Khan, Yaqub Khan, along with the *mullah* and the other men of the village talked about the Communist officers who were plundering the villages, not only to loot, but to search every home for *Mujahedeen* to capture and kill them.

Hajji and Yaqub, as Khans of their village, were responsible for getting their families and other villagers to Pakistan. That night, after coming home from the mosque, Yaqub Khan went and spoke with Nur Gul's father, to discuss sending their families across the border.

This presented a great opportunity for Nur Gul to come to Yaqub Khan's house freely to discuss his own personal issues and visit his wife, too.

The next day, Yaqub Khan and Nur Gul went to visit the jeweler friend and discuss the jewels they had left with him. They were hoping that the stones were real.

The jeweler had good news for them, "They are real! My dealer offered this amount." He wrote a figure on a piece of paper. They both looked and were astonished by how much they were worth.

Most Afghan refugees moved to Peshawar in Pakistan, taking their expensive items and antique possessions with them, or dealers would go to Afghanistan to collect valuable items from the local shops. Some of Afghans opened shops to sell these possessions of their countrymen. Foreign dealers took advantage of this opportunity and rushed to Peshawar to purchase these valuable items.

"My dealer asked if we have more because the buyers are interested," the jeweler said.

"We have a lot—" Nur Gul was about to say, when Yaqub Khan interrupted and said, "No, I bought those pieces from a man who needed money, urgently, to send his family abroad."

Nur Gul then realized that he would have spoken without thinking. Uncle Yaqub Khan was being tactful for the safety of the family. He was impressed by Yaqub Khan's negotiating skills.

The jeweler took them into the store's back room. From a large steel trunk, he took out bundles of money. He counted it, putting some aside to pay his dealer. He did not ask for any money for himself since Yaqub Khan was his best friend. Nonetheless, Yaqub Khan paid him, leaving a little extra as a gift for his good service. The jeweler put all the bundles in a burlap bag, like the ones people used for rice or flour.

"The time is not safe to take a bag of money home. What is your advice?" Yaqub Khan asked his trusted friend.

"You are right—it is dangerous to keep money at home. With all the bribes I am paying, I still fear for my property. I plan to leave soon. I can send your money through the network of *hawala* to Pakistan. When you come there, you can get it from me. Or if you know someone else, I will send it to him," the jeweler said.

Both men agreed on a network's receipt and the best friend would keep the money in Pakistan. They got a few bundles and packed them inside Nur Gul's large book bag, which teachers like him often carried. They went home feeling satisfied with the arrangements.

In those turbulent days, people were selling their homes, orchards, vineyards, and almost everything else they owned. A killing atmosphere was in the air of the entire country, created by the communist invaders. People wanted to get cash from their assets and possessions as soon as possible and send the money to a friend or relative in Pakistan. Soon after, they would leave the country themselves.

Yaqub Khan and Nur Gul, on the way home, had a long conversation about how to invest their treasure. "Son, among the villagers, we are already well-off, and people will not become suspicious about our findings. But still we need to be cautious because now we are even richer!"

"What should we do with our money in this time of war?" Nur Gul said.

"I will speak with our *mullah* about my plan, but not about our treasure. We could sponsor men and boys from our village to get out of the country before they get recruited or killed. We can open a big market in Peshawar and put many Afghan refugee boys and men to work to survive in a foreign land. This is just preliminary talk," Yaqub Khan said.

He continued, "That jeweler is my best friend, and I trust him as I trust my eyes. I will never be able to sell those jewels without his help, and I need more time to think."

For both families, a new life had started. It took Niki a few days to actually understand the events that were taking place. Her mind was still full of thoughts about the stable beating and the other horrors she experienced that full-moon night. Her twin babies in the corner, however, gave her the comfort she now needed.

Chapter 8

Days at the Creek

Day 1

Slowly, a few days passed. Niki was still sick and still very much confused when she woke up each morning in Amira's guest room. However, one morning, she felt noticeably better. She looked out her window at the pretty scenery of the backyard and saw the crooked creek, a few tall willows, and a huge mulberry tree. There were wild spring flowers in purple, red, and yellow scattered along the water's edge. Next to the creek was a raised terrace with a floor of large, flat, gray stones.

She saw Robia walking toward the terrace, carrying a big basket and a small transistor radio.

Amira entered the room with a jar of ointment for Niki's wounds. One side of Niki's face was still very sore and numb.

"I would like to go outside and sit with Robia," Niki said, pointing to Robia on the terrace.

"Next to the creek is Robia's favorite place. She always takes her work and her small radio and sits there for hours. She will be happy to have your company," Amira said.

"Give me some work to do for you," Niki said.

Amira responded with a smile and said, "You are still recovering from childbirth and need to regain your strength. Go, but do not stay long. When you return, be sure to take your medicine."

Niki covered herself with a shawl, and with a slight limp, she walked toward Robia. After a few steps, her head began spinning. She barely made it to the creek and had to sit down right away to regain her strength. Robia was busily working and did not notice Niki's approach.

Niki, after regaining some strength, soon said, "It is so pleasant to look at the sky, the sun, the creek, and all the spring flowers, and these willow trees. If I had strength, I would climb this tree, sit on top of it, and sing a song about being free from the horrible jail of my mother-in-law's house," Niki said. Then suddenly lowering her voice, she asked, "Doesn't she live next door?"

"Yes, but their house is on the other side of their large courtyard," Robia said.

Niki started to cough hard.

"For your cough, you need sweet boiled herbs. Come, sit here and lean against this tree. I will go fix some for both of us. I like it too," she said before running to the house.

Soon she returned with two mugs of the hot herbs. She said, "My father talks about moving us to Peshawar. Do you know anything about Peshawar?"

"I have heard about Peshawar. We had a neighbor whose fiancé brought her many gifts from Peshawar. She always showed her gifts to me. The one I loved most was a red velvet makeup box."

After a pause, she said, "Inside that box, there was a small mirror with a silver frame which had raised flowers on it, a compact of face powder, some red lipstick, and a small round box of rouge."

Robia wanted to know more about Peshawar, but Niki would talk only about her neighbor's gifts.

Robia thought, *Niki is so boring! What should I do if she comes every day to sit with me and disturbs me while I listen to my radio?*

Niki had something else to share with Robia. "Once, my mother said that Roya's family used to go to Peshawar to spend winters. It is warm during the winter. And they brought shawls as gifts."

"Who is Roya?" asked Robia.

"Roya is our relative. We grew up like two sisters, one in the village and the other in Kabul. She is going to school!" Niki said.

Robia looked surprised. "I heard that school is not good for girls. It makes them bold and schoolgirls will not make good wives or good mothers."

"It's not true. Roya, her sister, and her cousins are not bold. They respect people. They can read and write and, believe me, those Kabuli girls know how to recite the Holy Qur'an better than us village girls. And they know how to cook and clean."

Robia was getting disappointed being friends with Niki. Robia thought they didn't have anything in common and that Niki was just plain boring.

Niki was smart enough to notice that Robia was disappointed with her. To change the subject, Niki said, "I appreciate all your help, and I wish for you a handsome and good husband, like Nur Gul." She continued talking about Nur Gul and his kind brother. The last word brought a sparkle to Robia's eyes. Niki kept talking about them, especially about when they came to bring her gifts during the holidays. Soon, she got Robia's interest with typical teenage girls' talk.

Robia smiled and listened eagerly and asked many questions. At the end, she invited Niki to come every morning with her to the creek. Both girls seemed happy. Soon, Amira called them to come inside.

Day 2

The next morning, the girls walked to the creek. Amira went to the front yard, as usual, to supervise servants who were baking, cooking, and doing other chores. Every day, they had to cook plenty of food for people who came to visit Yaqub Khan. A few guests were frequent visitors in his guestroom for men, located in the front yard and separate from the main residence. Yaqub Khan took care of most of his business in this room.

Niki said, "The weather is warm and pleasant! I love to sit next to this creek and watch the water, trees and flowers."

"You speak like those girls who read the news on Kabul Radio," Robia said to Niki.

"We lived with my grandparents for a few years. My grandfather was a teacher. He taught religious studies and Pashto in a high school in Kabul. They said that he spoke rhetorically. He taught me how to recite the Holy Qur'an and to memorize Farsi poetry and special Pashto poems called *landy*. After his death, my mother continued to teach me what she had learned from her father. And I learned to speak Farsi well at our relatives' house in Kabul. We often went to visit and spent many nights with them. This made my mother and me to become close to our relatives and helped me to learn about city life."

She continued, "On winter nights, all of us would sit around the *sandaly*, eating dried fruits, and my grandfather would read to us or tell us stories. When he was reading poetry, my mother and I repeated the verses after him. My grandmother would be busy spinning wool, but her ears were with us, repeating the verses in a lower voice after him. Sometimes my grandmother also would tell us stories."

"What did you do on summer nights?" Robia asked.

"During summers, since my grandfather had to go to work early in the morning, we gathered early in the evenings in the gazebo next to a small garden and under the light of an oil lamp. My grandfather would read to us or talk with us there. When my grandfather was not home, my grandmother and later my mother would tell stories. I loved to hear those stories, again and again. My favorite one was the love story of the Prophet Yusuf," Niki said.

"Tell me that story, please, please," Robia requested.

Niki wanted to keep Robia's attention and eagerly began to tell the story of the Prophet Yusuf. Before telling this story, she remembered her grandmother and how she comfortably sat, straightening her skirt, then her shawl, and clearing her throat. Robia impatiently waited for the story to begin.

Niki began, "The Prophet Yusuf was the most handsome man in the world. Zulikha, the daughter of a prominent Egyptian, fell in love with him, and the women of the town started to gossip about her. One day, Zulikha, who was hurt by all this talk, invited them all to her palace. Servants served them apples with sharp knives. While the women were busy peeling the apples, Zulikha asked Yusuf to enter the room. When Yusuf entered the room . . ." Niki then started to cough badly without finishing the sentence.

"Yusuf entered the room, and then what happened?" Robia asked. For a moment, she ignored Niki's cough. Soon she felt bad, seeing Niki's face losing color.

After a long pause, Niki continued, "When Yusuf, the most handsome man in the world, entered the room, the women gasped at his beauty, and they cut their fingers. Those women never again blamed Zulikha for being in love with Yusuf. At the end, they married!" She finished the story with this happy ending.

Later, both girls walked to the house with Niki looking very odd in Robia's clothes, which were a couple of sizes too big for her.

"My mother said that if the village fabric woman does not show up one of these days, she will go to Kabul and will shop for you and the babies," Robia said.

Day 3

That morning, the village fabric woman showed up at Amira's house. She was a middle-aged woman, tall and strong, with a deeply sun-tanned face, like brown leather. She did not wear a burqa, but like many other village women she wore a large veil. She carried on her head a large bundle of her merchandise, being a variety of fabrics.

When Robia saw her, she said, "I should wish for something else! Yesterday, I mentioned this fabric woman. Today, she comes."

The fabric woman was also a source of news on what was occurring in the village's households and knew almost all the young girls' and women's names. She had a gentle behavior that helped attract her customers' attention and buy her fabrics. She even let them pay whenever they could.

She usually appeared before the holidays and after the harvest, at the end of the fall season. Sometimes she made special stops at people's houses to check if they needed fabric. She had attractive names for her fabrics such as "the shadow of a mountain." The most interesting name for one of her new fabrics, which made women and girls laugh, was *kakul-e* Ahmad Zahir. This alluded to the shocks of hair on the forehead of Ahmad Zahir, one of Afghan's most popular singers. The fabric also had rows of fringes.

That day, Amira—with the help of Robia—bought several fabrics for Niki and the babies and ordered more. When the fabric woman left, Robia took her new purchases to Niki and said, "I chose these for you. My mother is an excellent seamstress. She also trained me. We will make you beautiful clothes."

Niki touched the fabrics while admiring them and said, "They are beautiful, and you have a good taste. May Allah bless you!"

In the afternoon, the women got together to sew. They furnished the terrace with a cheap thick carpet made of cotton, two light mattresses, and a few cushions.

Robia was a strong young girl. She easily carried the heavy sewing machine from the house to the terrace. She placed the machine in front of her mother. Amira's plan that day was to sew two dresses for Niki and some for her babies, as well.

Amira cut one piece of the fabric at a time and handed it to Robia to sew on the machine. During the cutting and sewing, they worked in silence. From time to time, Robia broke the silence, talked, or asked a question. But from her mother, she got in reply only yes or no.

Finally her mother said, "One day, with all your talking while working with the sewing machine, you might run the needle through your fingers."

Robia laughed aloud. She loved to tease her mother.

Amira said seriously, "I have been telling you that a girl should not laugh so loud. People in the alley will hear you, which is not good for your father's and brother's reputation."

They kept working until the *muezzin* from the nearby mosque called for the late afternoon prayers.

Mother and daughter went inside to wash up before praying. Niki made an excuse and stayed in her place.

When mother and daughter returned, they brought some tea and cookies for a tea break. Robia took advantage of the time and started to talk. She told Niki, "That fabric woman always has a new story to tell, or the end to a previous episode."

"What was her story today?" Niki asked eagerly.

Robia replied, "The daughter of Wali Khan, who was raped a few months ago, died last week. The story was this—a farmer in charge of irrigation, on his way to work, heard a scream from behind a wall. He went to see what was going on. A man, who was struggling with a girl, saw the farmer and ran away. The girl had been raped.

She was crying, her hair was messed up, and her dress was torn. The farmer helped her put on her veil and then walked her home.

"To keep the farmer quiet, the girl's father gave him some money and warned him not to mention the incident to anyone. People said that her father and brothers found the man who raped the girl and killed him. He was a migrant who had come to work in the village during the summer.

"The girl died recently, and her family said that she died of pneumonia, but there was a rumor that her father killed her to save his family's honor because she was pregnant." Robia asked Niki, "To kill a girl because she was raped is a terrible thing, isn't it, Niki? It is an injustice."

Niki became deeply upset and cursed herself and thought, *Why did I ask about today's story? Every time I hear the word* rape *or* honor, *I shiver and wish to die. But I am glad that this family doesn't know about my secret . . . they only think that my mother-in-law does not like me.*

Niki was still struggling to digest the story she had just heard when Robia asked her mother, "Tell Niki the story of that gardener's daughter, Benafsha." She did not wait for her mother and went ahead with a short introduction.

"Benafsha, because of her beauty, married the son of a wealthy family. She had a magnificent wedding that we went to. Unfortunately, the morning after her wedding night, the husband sent her back to her parent's house. People said that she was not a . . . you tell the rest," Robia asked her mother.

"She was not virgin," the mother continued. "Because of the shame she brought to them, they moved to an unknown place. The story was that the Khan Pacha's son fell in love with Benafsha, just like in a fairy tale. They loved each other very much. The girl met him in his private garden. The young man promised to marry her. He even mentioned to her father that he was going to send his parents as suitors. Of course, her father did not know about their relationship. He thought that the Khan's son saw his daughter, was impressed by her beauty, and chose her to be his wife. But when the Khan's son mentioned his plan to his mother, she became furious. She had decided that her son should marry the daughter of the Khan of the neighbor's village, not the daughter of a gardener.

"Benafsha lived in silence with a broken heart, until one day a wealthy woman saw her. Impressed by her beauty, she wanted her son to marry her. Benafsha, disappointed by the Khan's wife's decision, married the new suitor. When the groom found out that she was not a virgin, he sent her back, thinking she was a leftover of somebody else," Amira said.

"Mother, if Benafsha loved the Khan's son, why did she not go *shingary*?" Then she explained to Niki about *shingary.* "I heard about *shingary.* It is when a girl loves a boy, poor or rich, and her family does not want that marriage to happen. The girl then runs away and takes refuge in the boy's house. The boy's family has to bring a *mullah* to marry them, which would show their honor to accept the girl and agree to marry her to their son. Am I right, mother?"

Amira responded, "Yes, but about Benafsha, probably she did not get a chance to escape to his house, or she was too scared. The gardener was certain that the Khan's son would marry his daughter. Since it did not happen, he then married his daughter to the son of a wealthy family. He did not kill his daughter, but he and his family moved to an unknown place."

Amira soon commented on her daughter's description of *shingary,* "Oh, wow, you have good information about *shingary*. Never try it."

All of them started to laugh.

Robia had another question. "Mother, tell me why, in our culture, a poor man can't marry a wealthy person's daughter? Or a poor girl can't marry a Khan's son?"

"My daughter, there is a good reason. The expectation of a wealthy girl would be high, and when the man could not provide what she wants, there would be problems. In my opinion, everybody should marry at their own level, as a Farsi expression says: 'Pigeon with pigeon, and eagle with eagle,'" Amira said, and continued, "but a Khan's son or a very rich person can marry a poor girl with fairy tale beauty, or if the young man's mother approves the marriage."

"Just like Niki, who has that beauty and will marry a Khan's son," Robia said and added, 'it is so good that Niki is here. We work and talk. Working with my mother, I have to be mute."

I wish you were mute, Niki thought about Robia at that moment.

Day 4

The next day, the fabric woman returned with the materials that Amira and Robia had ordered. Along with her merchandise, she also brought the recent news: The separation of the most controversial couple of their village.

"Did you hear that Qudus Khan's son separated from his wife after the death of his father?" the fabric woman asked.

"No, I did not, but I'm happy for him. He released himself from people's talk, even if it wasn't the fault of his wife," Amira said. The fabric woman added a few more bits to her news and then left.

That afternoon at the creek, Amira and Robia sewed more clothes and many diapers for the babies. To make diapers, Amira started to cut the fabric in triangular shapes with many folds, and Robia ran the machine to secure the hem with big stitches.

"Mother, why were you happy to hear the news about Qudus Khan's son?" Robia asked.

"The boy and the girl were victims of Qudus Khan's dirty ego," Amira said.

"Separation isn't shameful in our custom?" Niki asked.

"Their story is different. Qudus Khan, whom I am sorry to say had the title of one of the heads of our tribe, was a notorious homosexual. His gay boyfriend lived in his house for many years. Qudus was very rich and often went to famous restaurants in Kabul and took his gay friend with him, without shame. His gay friend's name was Jan Aga. He was not an attractive man.

"About twenty years ago, Qudus Khan married. He also let Jan Aga marry. He built him a small house in a corner of his big orchard. He was still his favorite. They have children the same ages. Jan Aga's wife has an ordinary face, and his older daughter got her father's looks, being tall, heavy, and not attractive.

"Qudus Khan's wife is a beautiful woman, a relative of ours. Sometimes we visit each other. Most of her time is passed in the kitchen. When I visit her, I go sit there with her. She is like a flower in the middle of smoke, working hard, silently, and never complaining, which is a sign of her nobility.

"Jan Aga's wife is confused, not knowing whether to be a servant or a part of the family. Sometimes she comes and sits with us and joins our conversation, and at other times, she sits next to the door, where servants are supposed to sit.

"Their children grew up together, and all of them called Qudus Khan, Khan Baba. A few years ago, Qudus repented of being gay and accepted Jan Aga as a family member.

"Last year, we attended the wedding of Qudus Khan's son and Jan Aga's daughter. The wedding was in a big hotel in Kabul. Many of the Khan's relatives, high-positioned people in the government, and his friends, were invited.

"When the bride and groom came in, people felt sorry for the handsome, slim, young boy, who wore a Persian fur hat and a black suit, being a typical rich village man's outfit. He looked embarrassed, walking next to the tall, huge, and unattractive bride. The groom was not embarrassed at the bride's appearance. He was embarrassed of her father. After his marriage, he never associated with his friends.

"Today, the fabric woman said that the union of these two young people who grew up in a strange environment had ended. The young man told his wife that he did not want to stay with a woman whose father was sleeping with his father. He told her it is not their fault, but he was not able to continue this kind of life." Amira continued, "I have never understood how rich gay men can bluntly have a gay friend, but the poor people get killed by other people if they are discovered to be gay. We call a gay person *gumrah*, a person who goes off the straight way."

Day 5

That morning, the weather was windy, but the sky was clear with bright sunshine. The water of the creek was high, and the wind made it wavy. The reflection of the sun seemed as though thousands of shiny stars were moving up and down on the water tops.

Niki and Robia were at the creek when Amira came and told them, "Today you have to make some cookies for Shah Gul. Tomorrow I am going to visit her because, since she broke her leg, I have not seen her. She might be wondering why."

Niki, who shivered when hearing Shah Gul's name, followed Robia, who went eagerly to the kitchen to get the ingredients for the cookies. In the kitchen, she noticed that Robia was humming.

Probably Robia loves to make cookies, Niki thought.

Soon they returned to the creek to begin their work.

"For the beautiful fabrics that you chose for me, I wish you get all blessings. You have very good taste, and how come you know the names of all the fabrics?" Niki said.

"Whenever my parents go shopping, they take me too. My favorite bazaar is Pul-e-Bagh Omoumi in Kabul. Have you been there?" Robia asked.

"Yes, many times, but I never shopped. My fiancé's family shopped for me. You know that I was engaged since I was nine years old. They provided me with the best. My only problem was with the shoes. They were either too big or too small. My mother would say, 'If your shoes are big, put some cotton in front of them, or if they are small, they will loosen up after wearing them for a while.' It never worked for me. I always had blisters on the backs of my feet. I would love to, one day, go buy shoes for myself."

Robia was impatiently waiting to show off her shopping expertise.

When Niki paused, Robia said, "Last year, several times, I went to Pul-e-Bagh Omoumi shopping center with my mother and my aunt for my cousin's wedding. My father accompanied us. We stopped at my favorite big fabric store, owned by one of those Hindus who wear big turbans. People call them *Lawla*. Their shops are full of colorful fabrics. Going there, I feel like I am going to *Jashin* for its Independence Day festivities. When they learned that we were having a wedding, they put mountains of fabrics in front of my mother and my aunt to choose from."

"What did you buy?" Niki asked.

"My mother, as an older sister, was in charge. She chose a white satin fabric with raised flowers called *toss,* a famous product from India, for the wedding dress. A plain white satin fabric would be chosen for *shalwar*, and white chiffon with small golden paisley prints for the veil. For the *nikah* ceremony, the color for the dress, veil, and shawl is supposed to be green. It would oftentimes be made with a fabric with a design called the shadow of a mountain. There would be a green shawl, white *shalwar*, and green lace for the veil, plus some extra fabrics for dresses for different occasions and for around the house. In addition, my mother picked some fabrics for the bride's mother, sisters, sisters-in-law, and aunts as gifts from our side," Robia said.

"In Kabul, a girl goes shopping with her fiancé's family to choose her wedding dress according to her taste," Niki informed her.

"That would be so awesome if I could go shopping and choose my own wedding dress, shoes, and everything," Robia said. Then she changed her mind. "But my taste would not be as good as an older women's because they have experience. It would be better that they pick for me."

"The Kabuli brides see pictures in a large book called a catalogue. It's full of pictures of brides wearing wedding dresses in different styles, and they say those styles change each year. From there, they choose wedding dresses. Brides in the villages still wear the same style from ancient times," Niki said.

"I just love wedding dresses and don't worry about the style," Robia said.

Niki and Robia kept talking about wedding ceremonies, and Niki shared her experience going to weddings which were taking place in the hotels in Kabul, with music, bands, great food, men and women gathering in the same hall, and girls and boys dancing.

When Niki stopped talking, Robia said, "See when we talk, the time passes fast, and work is done. The dough is ready, and now you can help put some designs on them," Robia said.

Looking at the creek, where the reflection of the sun made thousands of shiny stars on the water, Niki got her idea for her design. With the blade of a small knife, she designed stars, suns, and flowers on the round flattened pieces of dough.

Robia liked the designs and said, "The designs of our traditional cookies have always been small circles, triangles, or squares."

When Niki finished designing the cookies, Robia arranged them with much care in large flat baskets. Niki noticed she kept showing lots of interest making cookies for the next-door neighbor. At the end, Robia took them to the baker woman in the front yard.

Those cookies with different designs looked strange to the baker woman. "Young rich girls!" the baker woman said, shaking her head.

Day 6

This morning, Amira used her good brass tray, with a famous design from Kandahar, for the cookies. She liked the girls' new designs and left to see Shah Gul next door.

"What took you so long to come and see me?" Shah Gul asked with a complaining tone, putting her hand on the cast on her leg. After greeting each other, she asked with curiosity, "The fabric lady told me that you have a guest, and you bought her lots of fabrics. Who is she? And when should I invite her?"

Amira was about to stutter but calmly responded, "One of my cousins came from Jalal Abad. She has a cold, otherwise she would come to say *salaam* to you."

"Which one?" she asked and again did not wait for the answer and continued, "it is not good that your guest came from far away and you did not let me know, so that I could send her some food and sweets."

Sabro brought tea with fresh butter, cheese, bread just out of the oven, and cookies with traditional village designs on them.

While having tea, Amira wanted to be polite, as it was usual to ask about the family members. Calmly, she asked about everyone, and finally asked, "How is Niki?"

"Nur Gul took her to visit her mother," Shah Gul said, offering more cookies to her guest, to change the subject.

Sabro kept coming into the room to fill the cups with tea. Finally, she came and sat next to the door. She now was a middle-aged woman, with countless wrinkles on her face and a couple of missing teeth. Her appearance described her hard life. Part of her tangled, faded henna-colored hair hung from under her veil, showing that she was not taking care of her appearance. She was staring faithfully at Shah Gul, with a faint sign of feeling sorry about her broken leg. Amira knew her from an early age, working at Shah Gul's house.

Amira remembered that whenever Shah Gul was sick, she talked about it with exaggeration; but this time, she did not talk about her broken leg, why it happened, when it happened, or even how much it hurt. Instead, she talked about a different subject, such as "Sabro's daughter is going to marry a rich merchant. Sabro, you tell us," she commanded.

Sabro, with a big grin, did a long talk about her daughter's rich suitor. At the end, she added, "My wish is that he never beat her up and break her teeth, as my cruel husband did to me."

When Amira was ready to leave, Shah Gul complimented her cookies with different designs of moon, sun and stars and asked, "Did Robia make these cookies?"

"Yes, Robia did the dough, but my guest made the designs. She helped, even though she did not feel well," Amira said, not wanting to give all the credit to her daughter.

"*Masha-Allah*, next time, bring Robia with you," Shah Gul said. They said good-bye.

When Amira came home, Niki and Robia were anxiously waiting to hear about her visit next door.

"Did she mention my name?" Niki asked.

"You probably learned from Robia to ask questions before I start to talk. Yes, she said that you went to visit your mother," Amira said with a kind smile.

"What about the cookies? Did she like them?" Robia asked.

"Yes, she complimented on the designs of the cookies." Then she asked, "What did you do while I was gone?"

The girls showed off their unfinished handmade vests they were making for the babies.

While Amira went next door, Niki and Robia tried to sew something different for the baby girls. They talked and they worked.

Robia asked Niki, "When you were a little girl, did you play with dolls?"

"Yes, a lot. My grandmother was very good at making dolls out of cloth, and my mother helped to make dresses for them. I loved to dress my dolls and play dolls with the neighbor girls. We sent our dolls as guests to spend nights at friends' houses, and their mothers made parties to celebrate the dolls' weddings. The dolls' weddings were for women and girls," Niki said, and then asked, "What about you?"

"My mother made many dolls out of cloth for me too, and I also had one made of porcelain that my father bought me in Kabul," Robia said.

"Roya, my friend and relative in Kabul, also had several porcelain dolls. In Kabul, they call a porcelain doll *gudi chini*. We played with them, and she loved to play with the dolls that my grandmother made for me. She made several cloth dolls for Roya also. Aunt Safia, Roya's mother, gave me a *gudi chini*, but we kept it as a decoration on the shelf. I never played with it."

The girls, thinking about their dolls, continued sewing vests for the twins. Robia cut two pieces from the fabrics, one green and the other a golden color. Niki flattened cotton to put between the outer layers. They waited for Amira to finish them because the girls had never sewn a vest before. Since Amira was very skillful, the girls put their work away and spent the rest of the time talking.

When Amira came home, the girls showed her the still unfinished vests. She liked them, and something came to her mind. She sent Robia to the kitchen to supervise the dinner. Her father was expecting a few guests from Kabul that night. Amira said that she would finish the vests.

When Amira started to make the squares, she told Niki in a lower voice, "I am going to make small pockets in some squares where I am going to place a few pieces of jewelry. Make sure that Robia does not know about them. You must keep an eye on the vests."

Amira repeated, "Make sure you don't show them to anybody. I will only tell Yaqub Khan and Nur Gul about them."

Amira had safely kept many of the jewels found by Niki, deep in her pocket. She carefully got them out and with great attention, she sewed them inside the vests. Before dark, two cute handmade vests were ready for the baby girls.

Day 7

The weather was now getting warmer. After Robia had finished her work around the house, and Niki had taken care of the babies, they went to the creek to finish their sewing jobs. To quench their thirsts, they took with them a cold yogurt drink made by churning the cream out of regular yogurt and adding a bit of mint.

"Are the vests finished?" Robia asked Niki.

"Yes, with Aunt Amira's touch, they look very cute. The babies will wear them on the day of our journey to Peshawar," Niki said.

When Amira joined them, Robia asked with a typical teenage girl's excitement, "Now tell us, what was going on at Aunt Shah Gul's house?"

"Why are you so interested about what was going on at her house? But there was news! Sabro's daughter has a rich suitor, a merchant, who will pay a big bride price and buy her a gold *chamkaly* with bracelets. Sabro said that in her generation, her daughter would be the first to have real gold jewelry!"

"What's so good about her daughter?" Robia asked.

"She is young, and she is available for an older man who pays a large bride price. A relative of Sabro made the arrangement," Amira said and added, "I feel sorry that the girl is so young. Sabro said that her stupid daughter is not happy and begged her not to force her into this marriage. Sabro kept telling her that if she misses this opportunity, she will marry a poor man and will live in a hut, suffer poverty, and her husband will beat her often, like my older daughter Shreen."

"Rich old men don't hit their wives, do they?" both girls asked.

"It depends on the girl's luck," Amira said.

"I'm glad that we aren't poor so that you would not force me to marry an old rich man for the money," Robia said laughing and joking with her mother, "Please arrange my marriage with a rich man—" Before Robia finished talking, her mother interrupted her.

"Stop! In our time, it was embarrassing to talk with a mother about men, but nowadays girls are no longer shy."

"Mother, tell us that you have been lucky. You married a man who has all the best qualities: a good husband, not much older than you, very handsome, and he did not get another wife like some other rich men," Robia said emphatically.

"Knock on wood! Because there is an expression that says, 'the husband, the face, and the hair are not faithful!' A husband might get another wife, a face gets wrinkles, and hair turns gray—or a person goes bald. Yes, I am very lucky," Amira said.

"Did you have a bride price?" Robia asked.

"Yaqub Khan's family asked my father how much he wanted for the bride price. My father said that the bride price is like selling a daughter, and he did not ask for it. I remember that one of our farmers, for his daughter's bride price, asked for ten sheep," Amira said.

After a pause, she continued, "Unfortunately, this practice still continues, to exchange daughters for almost anything. It is because of the poverty. Another tradition, which I do not like, is *badal*, even though it sometimes turns into good marriages."

Badal is to exchange daughters. You give your daughter to my son, and I give my daughter to your son or to some other member of the two families.

"Tell us about *badal*. Is it a bad or good arranged marriage?" the girls asked.

Amira replied, "I have heard both good and bad stories. Let me tell you first my good story about *badal*: Hajji Rahim, a neighbor of ours, a respected man among the village elders, had an older girl who was not pretty and a son who was handsome and had finished the military academy.

"Hajji Rahim, with another man of our village, arranged *badal* for their children. The other man's son and daughter both were very good-looking. People in the village were surprised by this arrangement, and they wanted to know the other man's son's reaction. The young man accepted his father's decision with a lot of respect to marry the older and not-so-pretty girl of Hajji Rahim.

"But the sister of that young man was a good match for Hajji Rahim's son. The marriage ceremony for both couples took place on the same night, and the girls moved to their new homes.

"Years passed. During those years, the Hajji's daughter gave birth to only one child, lucky to be a son. She stopped giving birth because of her age, but the younger one had many children.

"The Hajji's son-in-law always expressed appreciation for his fortunate marriage and praised his wife for her wonderful personality and qualities. All four of them had happy lives."

Amira paused and then continued her story, "Now, let me tell you about the not good *badal* arrangement. There were two sisters-in-law who were also close friends. Both had two children, a boy and a girl. To perpetuate their friendship, they engaged their children. They had a big children engagement celebration and sent gifts to the girls. One girl's name was Nazifa, and the other was Anar. Nazifa's mother died after the engagement.

"When they grew up, Nazifa became a tall, thin girl with olive complexion. She resembled the gypsy girls who came to the village, which was not the ideal choice. She was smart for a village girl and a bit bold.

"But the other girl, Anar, had a typical village face—radiant and round with rosy cheeks, on the plump side and very quiet. When she laughed, it made her big bosom go up and down.

"When the boys grew older, they attended school in Kabul. They were the new generation of the village who did not wear turbans and *shalwar kamis*. They met girls in Kabul going to school and wished to marry them. But they had been engaged when they were little boys, and it was disrespectful to leave a childhood fiancée and marry someone else. They could marry another girl but had to marry the fiancée too.

"It happened, rarely, that someone did not want to marry a childhood fiancée, which would damage both families honor, especially the girl's status, and nobody would marry her unless somebody's wife died.

"Finally, it was time for them to get married. The wedding celebrations took place in the grooms' houses. Around midnight, after the celebration, each family escorted their bride to their new homes.

"Nazifa's story was this: In the morning of the wedding, when her mother-in-law went to check on the bride's virginity, she saw no blood on the handkerchief, which the bride was supposed to use to clean her blood with. The mother-in-law furiously went to her husband and told him that their daughter-in-law was not a virgin.

"The father-in-law became angry. He thought his family had lost all their pride, picked up a small axe with a long wooden handle, and went to punish the bride. He beat her with the handle of the axe and locked her in the stable for several days.

"The poor girl slept in the corner of the stable, and they threw her some food and water. When her relatives heard about it, they interceded and let the young woman go free.

"Nazifa's father heard about his daughter's situation but did not show any reaction. He waited for the right time to get his revenge.

After nine months, his daughter-in-law, Anar, gave birth to a son. The baby had an extra skin on top of his scalp caused by a deformity.

"When the grandfather saw the newborn baby, he grabbed him, held him to his chest, and walked nervously to his daughter's mother-in-law. When he reached her house, he placed the small tiny baby in front of her and her husband, saying, 'This is your daughter's product.' 'No, this baby is the product of your son,' Anar's mother said.

"A big fight broke out between them. The man who brought the newborn baby took advantage of the time and beat up his daughter's father-in-law, injuring him badly, remembering that it was he who had beaten his daughter with an axe and locked her in the stable. People around them got involved and advised the grandfather to send the baby back to his mother and to take him to a hospital in Kabul. After a few months, the baby died.

"Anar told her friends, 'This was the hardest moment in my life, when my father-in-law took my baby and left the house angrily to show his scalp to my parents. I loved that baby and wanted to hold him forever in my arms!'

"Many years passed, and Anar and her family now live in the village. They have several children. Nazifa loved Kabul and encouraged her husband to find a job there. The family eventually moved to Kabul, bought a big house, and gave the best room to her mother-in-law and father-in-law, as it is the custom to respect the elders and earn the husband's heart. They live happily with many children."

Amira ended her story and then added, "Nobody knew why Nazifa was not a virgin—even her husband kept quiet. People assumed that her husband slept with her while they were engaged, which still was taboo."

Robia said, "The good thing about childhood engagement is that the boy and girl meet and get used to each other."

"Did you see uncle before your wedding?" Niki asked.

"Oh! No, no, no! The first time I saw him was on our wedding night, during the *ainamusaf*."

Niki mentioned the word *ainamusaf* several times and said, "I always loved this traditional marriage ceremony when on the wedding night, the bride and groom would see each other in the mirror. Unfortunately, we did not have it." Then she asked again, "Isn't it for many grooms and brides to be the first to see each other in the mirror on their wedding night?"

"Yes, many girls and boys in the villages would have arranged marriages and would not see each other until the wedding night. As I saw Yaqub's face for the first time on our wedding night," Amira said.

"Who made the arrangement for you?" both girls asked.

"At a wedding, Yaqub's mother saw me and liked me. They are distant relatives," she said.

Amira, eager to talk about her lucky marriage, continued. "One day, those relatives, and a few elder members of the family, came to our house to ask my father for my hand for their son. My parents were happy to find their daughter a husband from a good family. They did not ask my opinion! They gave their consent. But later on the wedding night, during the *nikah,* a male relative, as a witness, came and asked if I agreed with this union. I said yes."

"If a girl isn't happy, can't she say no? It is a sin?" Robia asked.

"In our custom, the parents make the decision for their children, whether they are happy or not. It will bring shame to the family if a girl or a boy says no to their parents' decision. But in Islam, for a girl and a boy to get married, their agreement is required along with the consent of their parents," Amira said.

"Tell us about your engagement," the two girls asked.

"As is our tradition, after his family came to our house many times, finally my parents agreed to engage me to Yaqub, even though they had already made up their minds on that first day they came. Finally, one day, they stayed longer. My mother served them tea and gave them a tray of sweets, a sign of my father's agreement, and my father said yes. When they left, my mother came to my room and told me, 'You are engaged, and our dreams have come true.'"

She added, "I believe the arranged marriage is wonderful because the parents would choose the best for their children." Aunt Amira's voice had a deep echo of happiness and pride.

"Tell us, how many times did they come to your house to ask for your hand?" the girls asked.

"Coming to the girl's house many times, to ask for her hand, brings much honor to the family. Therefore, they came countless times. And each time they repeated the popular expression, 'Accept our son as your slave, or we will come to your house until our shoes turn as thin as the skin of garlic to obtain your consent,'" Amira said proudly and continued, "These two phrases are formalities which should be used on these occasions."

"They really came many times? But what about the word *slave*, what do you think, mother?" Robia asked.

"Of course, this comment is part of the formality by the suitors. It's just a word," Amira said.

"For many people, that word means the opposite, the girl becomes the slave," Robia said.

"Did you have a bride price?" Niki asked.

Amira proudly answered as she always did when asked this question, "My father always said that the bride price is like selling a daughter."

"Since your father did not ask for the bride price, what did they put on the tray of sweets when they returned it?" the girls asked.

"Yaqub Khan's father, as a token of appreciation, returned the sweet tray with twenty gold coins on it! That was a lot."

Niki wanted to know more about this tradition and asked, "Tell us about the tray full of sweets for the boy's family."

Amira said, "To give a tray full of sweets to the boy's family means the parents of the girl agree with the arrangement. Then the boy's family, as much as they could afford, would freely place money, gold coins, or jewelry on the tray as a token of appreciation and return the tray to the girl's family. In the wealthy families, they would spend that money to buy items for the girl's dowry.

"My mother had the village jeweler make a necklace, earrings, and bracelets out of coins for my dowry. I went to my husband's house with a spectacular dowry. My parents also bought me many clothes and jewelries," Amira said.

"Mother, how long was your engagement?" Robia asked.

"We were engaged for at least five months. For the holidays, they sent me gifts. My best gift was a small watch. None of my friends and cousins had such a thing. Besides the holidays, whenever his mother came to visit my mother, she brought me gifts and sweets," Amira said.

"Aunt, tell us about your wedding and your wedding dress?" Niki asked.

"I had a big wedding because Yaqub was the only son. The gate was open for the people in the village and a popular country singer,

Beltoon, with his band entertained. Young men were shooting in the air to celebrate Yaqub's wedding.

"My dress was light purple with raised golden paisley-printed satin. My veil was light purple silk, and my *shalwar* was light purple satin. I had gold *pizzar,* one of those traditional Afghani shoes made of fine leather embroidered with gold silk threads, and I wore a green shawl on my shoulders. My mother-in-law gave me her gold *chamkaly*!"

Niki, imagining Aunt Amira in her wedding dress, asked, "What was the style for the makeup?"

"My mother's cousin took care of my makeup. She put on my face a white powder mixed with water, rose-colored circles on my cheeks, red lipstick, powder from a grounded black special stone as eyeliner to darken my eyebrows, sprinkled silver powder on my forehead, and small green and red dots which were artificial tattoos in the shape of the moon, stars, and dots along the arches of my eyebrows. A day before my wedding, my aunt braided my long hair in many strips, which took a very long time."

She continued, "They gave me a designated place to sit, decorated with expensive fabrics. That night, I felt tired, sitting for hours, worried what the groom would look like. Hundreds of thoughts crossed my mind. "

"No doubt you were a very beautiful bride," the girls said.

Amira blushed and said, "My mother-in-law and the other women recited short verses from the Holy Qur'an to keep the evil eyes away. According to them, I was a very beautiful bride.

"Everybody was waiting for the groom to return from the family cemetery. The groom with his friends and a little boy of a close relative, dressed as his best man as it was our custom, was supposed to go on horseback to the family cemetery to pay respect.

"When they returned from the cemetery, in the men's hall the *nikah* was performed. A loud recitation from the Holy Qur'an filled the room. After that, a male relative from our side, as the bride's representative, came, and asked for my consent. And I had to repeat three times, 'Yes, I agree.' He returned to tell the news that the bride said, 'She agreed." The *mullah* recorded on the marriage certificate that Yaqub Khan, son of Doust Muhammad Khan, and Amira, daughter of Adam Khan, agreed to this marriage and that Yaqub's father offered them, a big *haqumahr*, one of his apple orchards.

"I agree with a big *haqumahr,* which is security for a woman in case of divorce or, God forbid, death of the husband.

"My father appreciated Yaqub's father's generosity and said that he was fine with the Islamic Law and the *haqumahr* of thirty Afghanis and a volume of the Holy Qur'an. Since the apple orchard was voluntarily offered from the groom's father, it was recorded in the marriage certificate next to the original *haqumahr*.

"After the *nikah* sweets were served, congratulations filled the air. Women started to dance and sing special songs for the occasion."

Amira continued to talk, "Soon, some children, running, entered the room to announce that the groom was coming to the women's hall! My heart started to beat faster, my palms started to sweat, and my head started to spin. My mother covered my face with my veil. The groom and his entourage entered the room.

"The ritual ceremony started. His aunt took charge, as she was the lucky woman who was supposed to perform the ceremony. In front of us, on an embroidered tablecloth, there was a volume of the Holy Qur'an, a mirror covered with a large scarf, a dish of henna, and a tray full of expensive *nukles*.

"When the groom entered the room, they immediately sat him next to me. My face was covered. Two women spread a large shawl over our heads. The lucky woman, the aunt, pulled my veil away from my face and handed us the Holy Qur'an. We took turns reading a few verses, kissed the Qur'an, and handed it back to the aunt." Amira took a little pause to clear her throat.

Robia impatiently said, "Mother, at the important part, you paused!"

Amira laughed and said, "I am not allowed to breathe?" She continued, "Then, the aunt held the large mirror under the shawl, and told us to look at the mirror. That time was special! Under the shawl, we looked at each other's reflections. He smiled, which meant he approved of me. I was too shy to look at him. However, I threw a quick glance at him, and I said to myself, 'Thanks to God. I like him!"

Both girls started to laugh. Amira embarrassingly said, "I was your age once!" She continued, "Then, they took away the shawl, and the aunt put henna on our palms for good luck, and extra henna on the groom's little finger to show that he was just married. Finally, she covered our hands with fancy small napkins for the occasion, so as to not spill henna on the bride and groom's outfits.

"The women showered us with candy, and the men who accompanied Yaqub threw money over our heads. The children would eagerly run to collect the coins. The groom and his entourage then returned to the men's hall.

"After the ceremony, even I was tired, but I felt relaxed and enjoyed my beautiful wedding dress, my jewelry, and seeing my friends all around me who were dancing and singing.

"Then dinner was prepared by the best cook of the village. As it was the custom, the gate was open for the village people to come in, eat dinner, and enjoy a country singer. The party lasted until dawn.

"My heart started trembling when I heard, 'It is time for the bride to go.' Outside the house, two men from the groom's family came with a *douly* or sedan which was a small carriage carried by men. My mother started to cry while several women walked with me and helped me get into the *douly*.

"Two strong men carried the *douly* on their shoulders, crossed our front yard, went through the gate, and walked to a carriage with two white horses. My two sisters-in-law were riding with me, and Yaqub was sitting in front, next to the carriage driver. Many other carriages followed us to the groom's house, which was this house. I have to say that I am a lucky woman, and I wish the same luck for both of you."

Robia and Niki were amazed to hear about that fairy tale wedding. With a sad tone, Robia said, "With this war, I won't have a big wedding, just like Niki."

"Don't lose hope," Amira told her daughter.

Day 8

Amira told the girls, "Today, I will spend all day in the house and in the front yard, preparing for the move to Peshawar. I'm giving you the job of sorting and folding the clothes and sheets, and then you'll have all the time to talk."

This morning, Robia and Niki made several trips bringing bundles to sort and fold. They started talking, keeping their voices low, while feeling the seriousness of the move to Pakistan.

Robia said, "I wish we would move to Kabul, which is my fantasy world. The streets are paved and people take buses from here and there and drive cars of different colors and sizes. The traffic lights . . . my father explained about the traffic lights. When it is green, a car should cross the street, and when it is red, a car should stop. I forgot what he said about the yellow one.

"There are rows of trees on both sides of the streets. Many times, I have passed the street in front of the king's palace, but now they call it somebody else's palace. I still like to call it the king's palace though. I loved to watch its tower with a large clock and the garden that one could see from the street through the large iron gate.

"My most favorite thing in Kabul is electricity. At night, everywhere you look there is light . . . light on poles on both sides of the streets, lightbulbs on top of the resident's gates, the bright signs of the stores, and much, much more. Before the war, every year when my father took us to *Jashen*, our Independence Day celebration, to Kabul, I loved to look at the colors of the lights decorating the streets, trees, and buildings. I wish that one day our village, which is not very far from Kabul, could have electricity.

"In Kabul, the houses are in different shapes and colors—some with angled metal sheet roofs and many with flat roofs—and tall buildings and restaurants where we eat when we go shopping. My father loves to take us to the restaurants, which have separate rooms for families or only for females. In those restaurants, my favorite thing is Kabul ice cream with pistachios and cream of milk."

Robia eagerly continued talking about Kabul, "There, some women and girls walk outside without a male companion and without veils. I wish one day I could go shopping with my friends, look around, and ride the bus back home, but I like to keep my veil on."

Niki kept saying, "Yes, yes, yes," meaning "I already know about all of the things you are saying." Finally, she asked, "Did you go to the zoo?"

"To the zoo? No, tell me about it," Robia said.

"I used to go with my relatives in Kabul. It's like a big garden, with cages for the different animals. My relatives knew the names of all the animals there, but I only knew about the lions, tigers, gazelles, and a few more. My favorite part was the birds section where I saw geese, parrots, canaries, and peacocks with their colorful feathers."

Niki took a pause then said, "But now, there is war in Kabul. I have heard that Kabul has been ruined. I hope my relatives are safe. It has been a while since I have heard anything about them."

Robia asked, "Tell me about your relatives in Kabul."

Niki, being proud of having family in Kabul and knowing more about the city life than most villagers, said, "They have a big beautiful house in Share Now in Kabul. The house has many rooms—all of them are covered with expensive Afghani carpets. The fabrics of the curtains, sofas, and chairs are made of thick satin. They have velvet and satin quilts for the family members and their guests. They even have down quilts!

"They eat in a separate place called a dining room where all of them sit around a big long table. They eat with forks and spoons. I remember those forks and spoons having beautiful designs on them. Can you believe that they were made of silver!

"We have small radios which work with batteries. Our relatives have a radio as big as a large trunk. It has a long wire hooked to the electricity, its top opens, and a gramophone is located there. They place a round black thing, called a record, into it, which makes music, and . . . I cannot explain it! You have to see it! Also, all their rooms have electricity. They use oil lamps only for decoration.

"Their recorder is one of the most amazing things in their house. It is like a small radio with two small reels. It turns around and makes music, songs, and even imitates people's talk. On the radio, you listen to a song, then you have to wait until they play it again, but with the recorder, any time you want to listen to a favorite song, you can turn it on and listen to it, over and over," Niki said and paused to make sure that Robia understood what she was talking about.

Robia did not understand about the gramophone or recorder and did not want to know any more about them. She quickly changed the subject and asked, "Does Roya have a favorite singer? Like mine is Beltoon, the very popular country singer."

"Yes, her favorite singer is Ahmed Zahir. I love Ahmed Zahir's voice too, but I don't understand very well the meaning of his Farsi songs," Niki said. She tried to remember other things in her relatives' house in Kabul to talk about, seeing that Robia wanted to hear more, even though she sometimes looked confused.

Niki wanted to give more information about the young popular singer and said, "Ahmed Zahir is the son of a prime minister! Unusual thing for a son of a prime minister to be a singer, as my relatives say."

Robia wanted to ask about Kabul boys but was embarrassed and waited for the right moment.

Niki kept talking, "Our relatives have two guest rooms, one for their guests from the city, which they call the salon, which is furnished with couches, sofas, tables, and a wall-to-wall shelf, which I love to look at and all the items placed on it. You know, even though their house is like my second home, I do not know the names of many of the things around their house.

"Their second guest room for relatives from the village is easy to describe. It is covered with a red carpet with black designs called elephant foot, dark red velvet mattresses on the floor with many cushions, and satin curtains. Those guests from the village eat in the same room. Before they start to eat, a servant girl or boy brings a ewer and a platter to wash hands. Then they spread on the floor a tablecloth to serve the food on.

"Their cook, under Aunt Safia's supervision, prepares the best food. I remember her advice to the cook that the color of your brown rice should be golden and the oil in the spinach dish should turn light green. Most of the time, they eat rice with meat and vegetables.

"They have late afternoon tea. I love their cream tea. This mixture should have a deep pink color, with sprinkles of cardamom and enough sugar to make the mixture sweet. It is poured into a fancy cup to drink. A spoonful of thick cream is added on top. The thick cream is made from boiling milk for at least eight hours! I remember, every time they made it, they would say, 'Fixing cream tea with thick cream is an art.'"

"Do you know how to make cream tea?" Robia, who loved cream of milk, asked.

"I have never made cream tea, but I watched them fix it many times. I can fix it for you if you want. I love the way they serve breakfast, lunch, and dinner. It seems that they have a celebration. One person always supervises setting the dining table properly, with a freshly ironed tablecloth and matching napkins. My mother embroidered all of their tablecloths and napkins herself!

"They cut the bread in squares and place them in a nice basket. In the village, we just tear the breads apart and throw them on the tablecloth. They have a world of proper manners, social graces, and classy ceremonies to go with their fashionable city tastes—" Niki could not finish because Robia interrupted her with, "Tell me about Kabul boys. I never liked Kabul boys. They speak too soft."

Nicki briefly answered, embarrassed to talk about boys, "They are very polite toward women and girls."

Quickly, she changed the subject and said, "When our relatives have weddings or other occasions, my mother, who is good at embroidery, works for them. She has embroidered for them many things—including quilts, covers, and cushion covers. Some of these embroideries took months to make, and it was a good reason for us to stay there and for them to keep us in their house. In reality, they have helped us a lot."

"How many sisters does Roya have?" Robia asked.

"She has one sister, Nasrine, who is abroad. I remember that Nasrine's fiancé came to their house freely without having the *nikah*. He took her to the cinema, restaurants, and to parks," Niki said.

Robia, wanting to be funny, asked her with a tone of making a joke, "You almost turned out to be a Kabuli girl. Did she influence you to become more intimate with your fiancé and get pregnant?"

That question ruined Niki's mood, but she said nothing. Instead, she kept talking about her Kabuli relatives' phone that they use to talk with other people outside, even in different cities; and their refrigerator, which makes ice and keeps the fruits and foods cold; and they also have running water in their kitchen and bathrooms.

Robia commented, "What a different world they have, and it sounds very strange to me, especially the way Kabuli women and girls dress. In Kabul, girls are walking with short dresses, bare arms, and bare heads. They dress like *kafers*, and probably, they are already *kafers*."

Niki replied, "It is not possible. They are good Muslims. While reading the Holy Qur'an, they cover their heads and they fast during the holy month of Ramadan. I think that dressing differently is the city custom. Girls are wearing short dresses or skirts with nice blouses and shoes. Also, Aunt Safia and her girls know how to sew with the machine. But for fancy clothes, they go to the tailor. According to them, their dresses are European style. Also the girls are allowed to put on makeup, cut their hair short, and fix their eyebrows before the wedding," Niki said.

"The Kabuli brides might look like middle-aged women," Robia said.

"Not at all. I was in Roya's sister's wedding, and everybody said that she was one of the most beautiful brides they ever saw. In Kabul, brides go to a beauty parlor. And—" Niki was interrupted again by Robia who blurted out, "I have been twice in a beauty parlor, once accompanied by my sister, and the second time I went with my cousin. You know that the village brides go to the beauty parlor to get perms on their bangs, and then braid the rest of their long hair at home."

Niki continued her talk,, "And for Nasrine's wedding, they took me with them to the beauty parlor. She got a style as they said."

"Tell me about the hairstyle?" Robia asked.

"The hairdresser washes and rolls the hair around small rolls, then makes the person sit under a big thing like a pot hanging upside down on a chair with hot wind blowing down from it to dry the hair. Then they comb the hair, tease the top part, and curl the bottom of the hair if they have long hair. Those beauticians know how to give many different styles."

"Tease the hair, why?" Robia asked.

"To keep the hair puffy," Niki said.

"Now I know why some women in Kabul have big heads!" Robia said laughing loudly and she immediately covered her mouth to keep her laughter down.

Niki said, "They fixed my hair the way Roya told the beautician. First, she curled my bangs, opened my braids, pulled them back, made a ponytail, and then curled the end of my ponytail with a long steel roll. I looked so different, and I felt so embarrassed."

"Does Nasrine have friends from the village?" Robia asked.

"Yes, many. Kabul girls love the village girls' friendship for their liveliness, jokes, talent of embroidery, and their loyalty. And it is known that village girls are fast learners," Niki said and remembered a joke to tell, "One day, in Roya's house, a few of Nasrine's friends from our village were there, sitting on the porch, talking and laughing. An elderly man, who was a relative, passed in front of where the girls were sitting. Sima Gul, one of the girls who had a happy spirit and was funny asked the old man, 'Uncle, how are you and where did you get that large shiny brass teapot?' 'What teapot?' the old man asked. Sima Gul laughed and ran into the house. When the older man went away, she came back to the porch. The other girls asked her what teapot she was talking about. He did not have any with him. She laughed and said, 'I meant his large bald head!' 'Sima Gul! If my father ever heard that you laughed at an older man, he will be very mad,' Nasrine said.

"My father would be mad too, but they are not here. I always saw my uncle with his turban on his head, and I was surprised to see him without it, and to know that he is bald. I am sure he will never know what I meant, otherwise, I would never say such a thing," Sima Gul said and kept talking and laughing.

"At that time, Sima Gul was engaged with a young man who was in the military academy. Her happy nature and her well-dressed ways expressed her comfortable life, until . . ." Niki paused.

"Until what? What happened?" Robia asked.

"Her fiancé was killed in a car accident, and her fiancé's family wanted to engage her to their younger son, only fifteen years old. As part of the family's honor, she was not allowed to marry outside of her fiancé's family.

"In another gathering, when we were at Roya's house, the girls were sitting in their usual place on the porch. Sima Gul was there too, with a pale face, upset about the death of her fiancé and her situation but still full of life. The girls were on the porch when Sima Gul's mother- in-law came with her younger son. After greeting them, they went inside. Soon the boy came out of the house.

"The boy looked younger than fifteen years old, with his blue eyes and blond hair. On his way back into the house, Sima Gul called to him, 'Hey, blue-eyed boy. Come say *salaam* to me.' The boy looked at her with a big grin and ran inside the house. Sima Gul, with a nonbelieving sound, said, 'I heard that his mother wants me to marry that doll, and he is going to be my fiancé! How could it be?' Then she laughed, ignoring the reality," Niki said.

"What happened to her?" Robia asked.

"The last time when I saw her in Roya's house, she was engaged to that blond, blue-eyed boy. She was not the same girl who was full of life. She was terribly quiet, and her face looked pale. She glanced at them and smiled with a closed mouth. Instead of sitting with her friends on the porch, she went inside and sat next to her mother-in-law," Niki said and continued, "That was her destiny!" Then she added, "I remember those days on the porch. Nasrine loved to talk about the films she saw in the cinema."

Girls were still talking when Amira called, "Lunch is ready."

Both of them were hungry and raced to the house.

When the girls returned from lunch, Robia who had been thinking about the cinema, anxiously said, "Let's talk about the cinema, which is a mysterious place for me. While going to Kabul, we always pass that big house with no windows with large pictures posted on the front wall. I heard from the older women that the cinema is bad for people's morality. Have you been there?"

"Yes, several times, and it isn't bad for people. In cinemas, people go to pass the time, like we go to visit the orchards or farms. There are cinemas showing Indian movies where they show famous dancers and also cinemas where they show American or European movies. Inside the cinemas, there are large white screens on which pictures move and talk. Understand?" Niki asked.

"Not really," Robia said.

"I understand you because the first time when my Kabuli relatives took me to a cinema, I was so scared! I remember we entered a large hall with rows of chairs filled with people. As soon as we sat, they turned the lights off, a loud noise came from the ceiling, and pictures came on the large white screen. I grabbed Roya's hand and asked, 'How long will we stay here?' A few *hush hushes* made me shut up, and Roya whispered in my ear, 'Don't talk,'" Niki said, the old fear still present in her voice.

She continued, "All the time, I sat next to Roya and felt suffocated. I closed my eyes and started to pray until I heard a song with a very soft and nice voice. I opened my eyes and saw that a girl was singing. I stared at her. Then a young boy came up on a motorcycle and took her with him, and they rode down a path ending at a beautifully manicured green lawn with many flowers. As I continued to watch, I forgot about my fear. During the intermission, I looked around and saw people dressed like foreigners—some middle-aged women with small head scarves and high-heeled shoes, carrying nice little purses. Boys and girls dressed exactly like boys and girls in the movie. Even their hairstyles were the same. At the cinemas my relatives go to, nobody wears burqa," Niki said, then added, "Last year, which was my last time going to my relatives' house, I saw they had bought a television. They call it TV."

"Now, what is that?" Robia said.

"It is like their large radio. You can see pictures of the people who are reading the news, singing songs, and playing in the dramas," Niki said and then added, "I wish one day our village could be like Kabul, with so much light and water in pipes coming into the kitchens and into the bathrooms, and *hamam* or public baths—"

While Niki was talking, Robia cut her off and said, "One day I wish to go to a *hamam*. Tell me more about it."

"It is like a big bathroom, almost ten times larger than your living room. It has no windows and has only one door. The hall is full of steam, and it is warm like a *tawakhana* our winter room in the village. There are two large basins full of hot and cold water. Women and girls keep filling their buckets with hot and cold water to wash themselves. Families and friends pick a spot to sit and wash themselves and their children.

"To light the *hamam,* several lightbulbs hang from its high ceiling. The first time I went to a *hamam*, it was a cold winter day. In Roya's house, the water pipes in their bathroom were broken and the women decided to go to a *hamam* nearby. We entered the *hamam*'s building. We stopped first in a small hall, and we girls changed to bath clothes, which are short, sleeveless, open-wide neckline dresses. The older women preferred to wear *loongs*, which is a large piece of cloth wrapped around the body.

"As soon as I stepped inside the *hamam*, I felt suffocated. That large steamy, soap-smelling, half-lit hall was full of children's noises, crying, and women talking loudly to hear each other. There, I was scared too, as when I went to the cinema for the first time. I started to pray hard and did not know what I wanted to pray for, or to be saved from what?

"However, I followed my relatives and sat with them in a corner. Soon, my eyes got used to the place, and I started to look around.

Near us were sitting a few other women with young girls and small children. A few young girls were playing next to the cold-water basin. Later I learned that they had a contest to see how many buckets of cold water they could pour on themselves without screaming.

"Some mothers were holding their children to wash them. When they got soap in their eyes, they screamed loudly, reaching for the sky. On the other side of us, there were two young women with red bath clothes, carrying new bath sets. They looked very pretty. I went near them to see their bath sets. Their combs and their hand and foot scrubbers had covers of pure silver, as I had heard about. Their bath containers were open. I stretched my neck to see inside it. There were a few colorful soaps, r*oushora,* which is a face cleanser, and crocheted wash gloves. They were new brides who were showing off their accessories.

"My eyes became really large, looking at everyone and everything at the *hamam*, I have to wash myself instead of watching others, and I was acting like a typical villager—as I was! I went with Roya to get the hot and cold water. My relatives used shampoo, but most women there used *gueeli sar shore,* the same mud we use to wash our hair.

"Aunt Safia asked for a *Kissamal*, a girl or a woman employed there, who, with a wash glove, scrubbed the women's bodies.

"When I left that day, I noticed my palms had hundreds of wrinkles on them because of the steam. The weather was very cold and fortunately my relatives had a car to take us home. On the way, Aunt Safia asked to stop at the butcher's shop to buy some meat and also to get a big bone for Seako."

"Who is Seaako?" Robia asked.

"They have a giant black dog. His name is Seaako. In Farsi, it means 'black mountain,'" Niki said.

"In our village, many people have dogs. If they are big, they call them dog or wolf, or puppy, if they are small and white. If they are from different places, they would call them with the name of that place, like *sagshamaly*, dog of the north side."

Soon Amira called them both inside ending their girl talk that day.

Day 9

This day, while wading in the cool and shallow creek water, the girls talked about the village girls' favorite places: the *goodar* and *ziarat*.

Niki said, "I told Roya about our favorite place, the *goodar*, a place near a stream or a fountain where rich village girls go to hang out with friends, but poor girls walk there to fetch drinking water. And some boys walk around, secretly watching the girls and choosing a favorite one. There are many love songs about visits to the *goodar*."

"Are you allowed to go to the *goodar?*" Niki asked.

"Yes, once in a while I go there to hang out with my friends," Robia said.

After many days of being together, Niki felt close to Robia and dared to ask, "Did you meet someone around the *goodar*?" Niki asked.

"Hush, keep your voice down. If my mother hears you, she'll get upset, but I'll tell you one day, at least not now," Robia said.

"After you and your family helped us and saved our lives, I vowed that I would be like a good sister to you and a daughter to your parents and serve them while I am alive," Niki said.

Robia responded, "I feel such a close bond with you too that I can tell you things that I would not tell my own sister. Now, listen! I met someone on the way to the *ziarat*, the shrine of Peer Baba, which is my mother's favorite shrine. My mother, with her friends once a month, on Wednesday, make some food for the poor, usually they make *halwa*. We girls, together with our mothers—or by ourselves—go to *ziarat* to pray and distribute the *halwa*. If we cannot make it, then my mother saves the *nazer*'s money for the next time.

"Let me give you a hint. One day, with my friends, I went to *ziarat*. On the way, a boy, whom I have known since I was a child, walked by me. Our eyes met for a few seconds and a pleasant feeling came to my heart. I got worried and pulled my veil over my face and continued walking. I almost fell twice thinking about that glance. Now he knows that on Wednesdays, I go to *ziarat*. Of course, he never comes close, but I still notice him in the crowd. He is so handsome," Robia said while she blushed.

Earlier, Niki had sensed a possible relationship between that boy and Robia. She recalled talking with Robia about him when they were making cookies for Shah Gul. Zalmai's mother and Robia also got along very well together.

"Isn't that boy Zalmai, Nur Gul's younger brother?" Niki asked. This disturbed Robia, but Niki continued, "He is not only handsome, but he is a good person too, as is his brother Nur Gul. I love him like my own brother. He always took my side."

Robia was surprised by this and did not hear the rest of what Niki was saying. After a few minutes, she said, "Now, you know about my secret. I beg you to keep it to yourself."

"Why should I keep it to myself?" Niki said.

Robia worriedly looked at Niki and asked, "What do you mean?"

"His mother is looking for a wife for Zalmai, and who will be better than you? I will mention this to Nur Gul," Niki said.

Robia hugged and kissed Niki on the cheeks and soon started to dance in her village style, holding two sides of her veil and shaking it in the air. Then, she started turning around and sang a popular village song with a low voice, "Go to Nangharhar and bring me a black dress with three or four fresh flowers."

The two teenage girls started splashing water on each other and kept playing "*abouba jan abouba, dasta gulim sharaba, sharable ma khordani peshe Hakim bordani* . . ." It is a play in which girls hold each other's hands crossways, and turn around singing those nonsense sentences—very popular among girls in towns or villages. It is like children's talk, without clear meaning. Probably in the old times told a story, but now it is only a tune, having lost its original meaning. The words are still beautiful, "O beloved, O beloved, my bouquet of flowers looks like wine! The wine is drinkable and could be taken to the governor . . ."

The girls kept singing and playing *abouba jan abouba*, and their veils were thrown to the ground. While turning around and singing, their pleated skirts moved in the air like an umbrella around them, and their long braids were swung left and right around their shoulders. Both girls forgot about the world around them.

"What is going on over there? Other sixteen-year-old girls are going toward maturity, but my girls are going back to childhood. Hurry, hurry, playtime is over," Amira called to them, thanking God to see the girls so happy.

Amira had been concerned about Robia, thinking about whom she would marry. She was a good girl and hardworking but not as smart as her older sister. Walking next to Niki, who had fairy tale beauty, poor Robia looked very ordinary.

When they reached the house, Robia passed the porch and entered the house in a hurry, but Niki started to cough hard. She sat on the stairs, thinking that her lungs would burst. This condition had happened to her several times. While sitting, she thought, *Robia told me her secret, but I will never be able to tell her my secret which is too shameful, too tragic and too . . . I can't even find a word for it.*

Thinking about Nur Gul, who knew her secret and understood her, gave her comfort. Niki vowed to do something good for Robia and her family for the good things they did for her.

Day 10

It was another beautiful late spring day. Robia and Niki walked toward the creek. After a few steps, Robia began running to reach the creek before Niki. Robia was thinking about how to start the conversation.

Robia called, "Niki come here and look at the schools of fish. It looks like they have fun traveling together. Where are they going? They always go with the direction of the flowing water. How will they know how to return home?"

Niki went closer to the side of the creek and watched the fish, in different sizes, moving fast. "I think when the water is calm, they will return home," Niki said with a big smile on her face. It seemed she had read Robia's mind.

"Last night, I told Nur Gul that you are a perfect candidate for Zalmai," Niki said.

"Tell me, tell me what he said," Robia impatiently asked.

"Nur Gul said that uncle Yaqub Khan's daughter is the best choice for his brother. And he is going to talk with his mother," Niki said.

"If I marry Zalmai, it will be like a love story with a happy ending. My wish will be fulfilled, but what about the mother-in-law? What if she treats me like you?" Robia asked, and then continued, "I am just talking, and my wish is too far to reach. And I am not sure that Zalmai even loves me that much to marry me. I am crazy about him. You don't know how often I think about him and how many times, I went back and forth to the rooftop to see him from far away. My love is the love of saints. I have never even touched his hands."

Niki said, "You are the best bride for him, so let's pray and vow some food offering for the poor that his mother gives her consent."

Robia was thinking, *What if Zalmai's mother does not agree with this union and has another girl in mind for her son?* Robia felt sick and went to her room for the rest of the day.

That night, Robia was praying and thinking about Zalmai and his mother's decision. She vowed then, that if her wish comes true, she will offer food for the poor.

Day 11

Robia went to the creek, sat next to the water, and looked at the fish, the wild spring flowers along its bank, the trees, and the cloudless sky. Today, she did not enjoy them as she used to. She now felt only a cold chill creeping into her soul.

She kept telling herself, *I wish I had not told my secret to Niki. If Zalmai's parents do not accept me as their daughter-in-law, I will feel humiliated. Then what would I do, cry? Hide myself? Play sick and not leave my room?*

Her thoughts stopped when Niki came to her and said, "I have news for you, which is worth a big reward."

When a person has good news to tell, the expectation would be to receive some sweets as a reward.

"Tell me, tell me, but keep your voice down. Sometimes my mother can hear me as if I am in the same room!" Robia said sadly.

"Shah Gul accepted what Nur Gul told her, and she even told him that after Aunt Amira visited her and took her the cookies with beautiful designs, she was thinking about her daughter for Zalmai. Tomorrow evening, they will come to propose," Niki said.

"Your designs brought me luck," Robia said happily.

Robia stared at Niki for a few seconds. Niki noticed that her eyes had changed from worry, to surprise, then to happiness.

Robia looked around and saw the blue sky now clearer than ever; the sunshine felt more pleasant, the water of the creek was in its calm cycle; and schools of fish, some the color of gold, were swimming together in slow speed. She even sensed that the wild flowers, in their variety of colors, were especially spreading good smells on the air. The face of Niki seemed more beautiful than ever, as if she was an angel of good news. The cold chill was now leaving her.

"Pinch me so I am not dreaming," Robia asked. The girls hugged each other and promised to be good friends forever.

While Niki and Robia were sitting by the creek, Nur Gul came to the front yard and briefly told Aunt Amira that tomorrow evening, his parents would come to visit and ask for Robia's hand for Zalmai. He then went out the gate, leaving Amira in a very happy new world.

Later, Amira, who was so impressed by the news, told the girls that tomorrow there would be guests from next door and told them what Nur Gul had said. Niki hugged Aunt Amira with great joy, but Robia ran into the house because she felt so shy in front of her mother.

"Niki, since the first night you came to my house, you have brought us good luck," Amira said and, with a smile, added, "I would like to keep you in my house forever, but you need to go home and be with your husband. I will find a way for Nur Gul to take you home and ask his mother to make peace with you. Tomorrow when the guests come, make sure you do not come out of your room and nobody should know that you are here. I am going to make the guest room for the men ready. Even they will not be able to see you," Amira said.

Day 12

It was a big day for Robia. She went early to the backyard and sat next to the creek, waiting for Niki to come. Soon, Niki came and sat with her. Both were excited. That day, Niki did not feel well and returned to her room to rest. Robia joined her mother to help and to supervise the servants with cleaning and organizing the guest room. They also prepared to serve a simple tea with cookies.

Around evening, Nur Gul's parents, with a few elder relatives, came to speak with Yaqub Khan. After having tea, Nur Gul's father told Yaqub Khan the reason for their visit. He asked Robia's hand for his son Zalmai.

Robia's father did not respond immediately, which was the tradition.

After that day, the gatherings by the creek did not happen, as often, for the women had more tasks around the house for the preparation of the engagement party, which was supposed to be only for close family.

The coming and going of the suitors, including Shah Gul, continued a few more times. Niki was happy for her friend, but at the same time, the thought of Shah Gul being at the same place with her, made her shiver.

One day, after they had decided to say yes to Zalmai's family, Amira organized a small engagement party and fixed a feast of tea with milk with different kinds of pastries, cheese, butter, kebab, and several more dishes for the occasion.

This time, the guests were accompanied by several young cousins of Zalmai, both boys and girls. Before serving the tea, Amira brought a decorated tray full of *nukles,* a large sugar cone covered with golden paper, and a scarf with golden tassels which Amira made many years before and had kept for Robia. The tray with all these items was the sign of consent to the engagement. The tray was placed in front of Shah Gul.

The guests congratulated each other, and after having tea, they left happily. The cousins took turns carrying the decorated tray on their heads, dancing while going next door. The engagement party and big wedding, because of the war, was cancelled. They spoke of performing a simple *nikah* soon.

After the guests left, Yaqub Khan and Amira went to their daughter's room.

"My daughter, you are engaged to Hajji Khan's son, Zalmai. It has been our wish to marry you to a good young man, belonging to a good family, and our wish is fulfilled."

Amira said, "Thank you, Allah, that my wish came true."

Mine too, Robia said in her mind, thinking, *Such a difference between my mother and me. I am more fortunate because my parents' wishes were mine too.*

Later, Yaqub Khan asked his wife, "Why don't we celebrate the births of our girls? We behave like people before Islam when they were ashamed of having daughters, until the Prophet Muhammad, 'peace be upon him,' showed a daughter's value by walking hand-in-hand with his youngest daughter, Fatima, and even called her Little Mother. Our *mullah* preaches about that, but when we have a girl, we become embarrassed and hide the birth. When our daughters were born, we did not have any festivities for them, we did not shoot our guns, but when our son was born, we especially had festivities for his birth and gunshots were fired into the air."

Then, with a voice that expressed a firm decision, he said, "I am going to change that when we will have granddaughters born in the family. I am going to celebrate their births and shoot into the air."

"I bet that you won't do it! With all the qualities you have, you have one weakness—you are a slave of our culture," Amira said.

At first, Yaqub Khan was not in agreement with her comment and said so, but soon took back his words and said, "I admit that you know me better. I do not think I will be that brave to celebrate the birth of a girl. People will laugh at me. It takes time to change people's thoughts."

"You fear that people will laugh at you? Let them laugh. I am afraid that one day you will do something wrong with your fear of being laughed at," Amira said to her sincere husband, in a joking tone.

"I agree that the situation of females is miserable in our culture. Look at Nur Gul's sick wife with her two little baby girls. They are hiding in our house—what can we do? We are prisoners of the old ways," Yaqub Khan said.

Amira worriedly told him, "In the past few nights, Niki gets very sick. I believe the medication has lost its effect on her. I will ask Nur Gul to take her home and ask his mother to make peace with the young woman and take her to the hospital because she is so ill."

Chapter 9

The Soviet Union's puppet government in Afghanistan made the atmosphere of the entire country bleak. Monster-looking helicopters were dropping bombs, hitting the unfortunate people everywhere. From unknown and different directions, weapons were being aimlessly fired many times day and night. Like all other Afghans, life was uncertain for Nur Gul and his family too.

He feared every minute for himself and his brother and whether they would be sent into compulsory military service to fight against the *Mujahedeen*. Their house was on the list at the checkpoint of their district to be looted, according to Shapoor, a nephew of Yaqub Khan's farmer. Shapoor was working with the government. After receiving a large bribe from Yaqub Khan, he prevented the looting and even promised to help them when they leave for Peshawar.

A majority of the villagers, including the farmers, had fled to Pakistan already. A few of them had joined the State Secret Police or Khad in Afghan government for higher pay, to spy on their own people. Nur Gul was suffering more because his sick wife was still hiding in another person's house.

When Nur Gul came to visit Yaqub Khan, Aunt Amira told him about Niki being sick and needing to go to the hospital and about the possibility of making peace with Shah Gul.

Nur Gul went to Niki's room. Seeing her beautiful face now sunken because of illness terribly upset him. He went home to convince his mother to let Niki come home, supposedly from her mother's house.

He walked straight to his mother's room. She was sitting on a mattress, sipping her tea. Seeing his mother's stubborn face, he almost became discouraged and backed off. At that moment, he remembered when, as a little boy, he had a way to get his mother's attention to agree with his wants. He would now indeed try his old trick.

He walked toward his mother, knelt in front of her, kissed her hand, cleared his throat, and started to talk about the war and the compulsory recruitment of young men to the military. He emphasized his fear of the government if they picked up him or Zalmai.

His mother's face reflected a reaction of deep worry.

"Now is the time!" Nur Gul said to himself, and he was about to mention Niki's name, when his mother surprised him by saying, "First, bring Niki home, to save our honor. Some of our relatives and neighbors, out of curiosity, are asking about your wife."

Nur Gul thought, *For Afghans, honor comes first! I was certain that me and my brother, being targeted by the Communist government, would make my mother worry more than bringing Niki home.*

His thoughts vanished when his mother said, "God forbid! If they take my sons to the military, I will die!" She said this in a sad voice, and then she continued, "When will we leave for Peshawar? I have to start packing."

"Soon. And mother, do not pack everything. Just put a few necessary things in a bag. When we go to Peshawar, Insha-Allah, I will buy you whatever you need," he said.

"May I take my heirlooms?" she asked like a little girl and continued, "God bless Yaqub to help us move to Peshawar."

Nur Gul's father shared everything with his wife, and therefore, she knew about the plan that Shapoor, the nephew of Yaqub Khan's farmer, would help both families pass the checkpoints on the frontier and facilitate their trip.

Suddenly, Shah Gul held her son's hands and with a motherly look, which had been her weapon to conquer Nur Gul's heart, asked, "Son, I want to hear the truth from you. Niki's child is not yours."

Nur Gul had expected to hear this question sooner or later. He rolled his eyes, moved his eyebrows a few times, and played with his fingers. Finally, with a tone full of sorrow, he said, "She was raped by one of those hashish smokers near the graveyard when she was accompanying her mother to go to visit her father's grave. On the way back home, they met a few girls from their alley who had food for the poor, and Niki started talking with them. Ozra began to walk on and asked her daughter to follow her when she finished talking. When Niki was late, Ozra thought that she must be coming with the other women and girls. She never learned that her daughter was raped on the way home from the graveyard."

Nur Gul made up that story and felt low telling a lie to his own mother, but he had promised Niki that he would never mention Baz Gul's name. He remembered what Niki had asked him, "I beg you do not mention Baz Gul's name to anybody because my mother will die if she learns what he did to me. You must guard my secret."

What Nur Gul said satisfied his mother. Shah Gul felt better that her son trusted her with his big secret, but deep down she was hurt, thinking, *gave birth to* a harami. *I had hoped even for a love child of Nur Gul.*

Nur Gul continued, "Aunt Ozra believes that the babies are mine. She thought that I had come to meet Niki and that she did not tell her about it." Then he asked, "Doesn't that help to save our honor?"

"I am so relieved that her mother does not know about it. It is obvious that Niki is not damned because Ozra would talk to her aunt to get advice, and the news would spread around," Shah Gul said. She then told Nur Gul, "Bring her and her baby." It seemed she did not hear babies.

"She has twin girls!" Nur Gul said.

For a second, Shah Gul closed her eyes and what crossed her mind was the night she had locked Niki in the stable. An unknown reaction of remorse, repentance, or fear attacked her. She believed that Nur Gul had saved Niki and took her to her mother's house to give birth. She asked no more questions.

When Nur Gul saw his mother in a pensive mood, he once again wanted to attract her attention. He finally said, "Dear mother,

I will do anything if you treat Niki better. She is very sick. We are Muslims—forgiving and forgetting is part of our religion."

His mother said, "Since when did you become a *mullah*? You have to promise me too that you will marry another girl and have a big wedding in Peshawar and fulfill my wish."

Nur Gul blamed himself for asking a favor.

Later that day, Nur Gul brought his wife home. Niki's once beautiful, radiant face was now colorless. Her clothes were new and neat, with a purple pressed veil. She was holding two tiny babies, trying to hide her difficulty walking. With great fear, she walked to her mother-in-law and bent herself to kiss her hands. She expected another beating and scolding but saw her mother-in-law motionless and silent, like a mountain of ice.

Nur Gul took Niki to his room and offered her his bed. To Niki, the quilt on the bed looked like the same down quilt she saw at Roya's house. She placed the babies on the bed, touched the quilt and the bed to make sure that they were tangible and real. To Niki, Nur Gul had always been like the prince in those folk tales that her grandmother used to tell. That night, Nur Gul seemed more valiant than ever to her, and she felt love and happiness.

Nur Gul was happy yet disturbed by the presence of the *harami* baby girls, "You need rest. I will go ask Sabro to bring you some food and tell my mother that tomorrow, I will take you to the hospital. Uncle Yaqub and Aunt Amira insisted that I should take you to the hospital as soon as possible." He left the room.

It was evening when Nur Gul returned to his room. He looked at his wife then asked, "Why is your face so sweaty? Do you have a fever? Do you have pain?"

Niki replied, "I have had fever for the past few days. Aunt Amira said that I might have after-birth sickness. I think that I need rest, and it will go away." That moment, under the light of the expensive oil lamp used in the Khan's house, her face now looked rosy from the high fever.

Later that night, Niki's fever went so high she began to have seizures. Nur Gul became worried and went to wake up his parents and Zalmai to ask for help.

Seeing her condition, they decided to take her to the hospital right away. Zalmai brought the car up to the gate. For security reasons, they very rarely used their own car. Nur Gul went over to Aunt Amira to inform her about Niki's worsening condition.

Zalmai got out of the car and waited. He smiled when he saw Robia and her mother finally coming out of the house to accompany Niki to the hospital.

Nur Gul carried his weakened wife to the car, noticing how little she now weighed. Shah Gul, limping, walked along with them. Seeing Amira and Robia going with Niki without her, she conveniently said, "If I did not have this cast on my broken leg, then I would also accompany you to the hospital."

Nur Gul's father, before leaving the house, put some money in his pocket to bribe the officers on the way if they wanted to make trouble. He feared for Robia's safety and wouldn't let her go with them.

"Send someone then to take Niki's mother to the hospital," Amira requested of her daughter who was not happy about being left behind.

The car slowly disappeared into the dust-filled air, gently piercing the gray light of the early morning with Zalmai driving.

Shah Gul walked back to her house, worried about her sons going to town, and that Zalmai was the one driving the car. "This whore has been trouble and has taken away my peace," she said. Then something crossed her mind, she paused for a few seconds and said to herself, "Since when have Amira and Robia become that concerned about Niki to accompany her to the hospital?" She answered her own question by thinking, "Probably as new relatives they wanted to show me how concerned they were."

Sabro was in the yard and walked with her to the house. Both went to see the babies, who were still asleep. Those baby girls being in the house still greatly disturbed Shah Gul. She went to her bed, thinking, *Two* harami *girls are under my roof! Two* harami *girls! If somebody learns about these babies, not belonging to Nur Gul, there will be a big scandal in the village*. She felt that her family's honor was even now in greater jeopardy.

Shah Gul made several decisions, changing her mind several times. Finally, she made her mind up and made a deal with Sabro, her faithful servant.

"Tomorrow, when the men go to morning prayer at the mosque, you take the babies to the mosque on the other side of the village and place them on the porch. Make sure nobody sees you."

At the end, she added, "These are innocent babies. Now go, feed them, change them, and put them to sleep."

While his father and brother returned home, Nur Gul stayed at the hospital. They told Shah Gul that Niki's condition was very bad, and tomorrow, after going to the mosque, they would again go to the hospital. When they asked about the babies, she said that they were taken care of and were asleep.

Chapter 10

Early the next morning, when Nur Gul's father and brother headed to the mosque, Sabro, who slept in the babies' room, started to prepare the twins for their unknown journey. Sabro saw the silver prayer charms around the babies' necks, with verses from the Holy Qur'an carved on them. She kissed the prayer charms, and fearing to take them off, she let them stay.

Shah Gul entered the room and approved Sabro's job of swaddling the babies in rugs. She promised Sabro a big reward and warned her to keep her mouth shut.

Shah Gul saw two baby's vests on a pile of clothes and told Sabro, "Take these vests and give them to your son's newborn."

Sabro snatched the vests and put them in her satchel and then left the house with the twin girls under her burqa. She walked quickly through the empty alley and headed on the long walk to the mosque on the other side of the village.

When she reached the mosque, she placed the babies on the porch and turned her back on them, never expecting to ever hold them again. At a safe distance, she stopped, looked back, and felt comfortable that nobody saw what she had done.

After walking a bit farther, and still being not too far away, a thought came to her mind. She immediately changed her direction and rushed back to the porch. She quickly picked the babies up, put them under her burqa, and headed to the only bus stop in their village.

The bus was waiting for the regular male passengers going back and forth from the village to Kabul. Sometimes a few women were among those passengers, which allowed Sabro to blend in the best she could.

She got on the bus and took a seat next to the window in the front row. The first four front seats were reserved for women. It was obvious that she was holding a big bundle under her burqa. Luckily that morning, no other women were riding the bus, which made it easier for her deception. In the villages, women knew each other, even wearing a burqa. However, she already had an answer ready. If somebody recognized her, she would say that she was taking her grandchildren to the hospital.

From the window, Sabro saw Nur Gul's father and his brother, both of whom were swiftly walking toward the bus. She held her breath, head down, and closed her eyes as long as she could before opening them again. She turned her head back and saw the two men sitting quietly in the back. They were motionless and were looking straight ahead to the necks of the passengers sitting in front of them.

She let her breath out and thought, *They are not coming after me. They are going to town.*

Sabro's improvised plan was to take one baby to her daughter, Shreen, who lived in Sheen Ghala Village, and take the other one to Kabul, to the daughter of a family whom she had known since childhood. Her father was their gardener.

Both babies slept peacefully all the way to Sheen Ghala Village, which was just a few stops away from Angur Dara Village, and only one stop away from Kabul.

When the bus stopped in Sheen Ghala Village, she fixed her *burqa* in order to see her way better. Holding both babies under the burqa was not hard for her because she often carried large baskets of fruits, vegetables, or handmade materials that way to sell in Kabul.

She got off the bus and walked quickly toward Shreen's little house, not far from the main road. She knocked on the door.

Shreen opened the door and let her in. Sabro entered the plain backyard, sat behind the door, and opened up her burqa. At the sight of seeing her mother holding two babies in her arms, Shreen gasped.

"One baby girl is for you," Sabro said with great excitement.

"A girl? I have always been telling you to find me a baby boy. Last time when I mentioned adopting a baby, my husband raised his voice and emphasized that the baby should be a boy!" Shreen said.

"Then, at least keep one of them until this evening when I return. I will take her back and leave her at the mosque. You have a goat. Feed her and pour some milk in a bottle and bring me a small spoon too for this one, and hurry, before I miss the bus," Sabro said.

Sabro with only one baby now headed to the bus stop. The bus was still waiting to get more passengers. She got on the bus. This time, all the seats for the women were occupied. She had to sit on the floor, next to the driver's seat. She never paid the fare on this bus, and the driver's assistant, who collected the fares, had always been nice to her. Sabro prayed for him again and again, "May Allah grant you a beautiful wife." The driver's assistant would giggle and let her ride free.

That day, she uttered her pleas in a lower voice. She feared being on the same bus with Nur Gul's family members, but the presence of other women and children made her feel less noticeable.

The bus moved on, heading now to Kabul. The bus reached its last destination and parked across from the Pamir Cinema, near the Kabul River. Sabro wanted to go to Share Now, about a one-hour walk away. She started to walk on the clean city sidewalks and past the cinema. On its wall, she saw a very large poster of an Indian movie star in a dancing position. Half of her waist was naked, and a man was holding her hand. "A shameless girl," Sabro said.

Next to the cinema, the street was divided in two sections with one going to the new part called Share Now. In Farsi, it means "new town." It was a section of Kabul with modern houses and freshly swept streets with rows of trees and flowers, where the majority of the elite and rich people of Kabul lived. The other street was going to the old part of the city, Jada-e-Miwand, named for a famous city in Khandahar Province.

She crossed the paved street and took the road along the river to Share Now. Before going much farther, she sat and leaned back against the raised half wall alongside of the Kabul River to catch her breath. She held the baby on her lap. An old man with a white beard passed by and, thinking she was a beggar, dropped five Afghanis in front of her and slowly walked away.

Sabro eagerly grabbed the money from the ground. Soon she was on her way to Share Now's bus stop. When the bus arrived, she got on the bus and sat in a seat, proud of having money to pay the fare.

When she got off she only had a block to walk. Soon she stopped in front of one of the better-looking houses. This was Safia's home. She knew to ring the doorbell and not to knock. She was let in.

Sabro had finally appeared with a baby girl. Khadija, Safia's sister, had been waiting anxiously for many years for an orphan to adopt. And now a child had appeared!

Both sisters were overjoyed with the baby girl and promised Sabro a big reward. Khadija asked her to come tomorrow to receive her money.

Sabro also told them that the baby has a twin sister. She told them about stopping at her daughter's house. My son-in-law does not want a girl. So, on the way back home, I have to pick up her twin and take her again to the mosque," Sabro explained."

Safia and Khadija felt sorry for the babies and asked Sabro to bring the twin sister to them as well. They promised Sabro even more money if she would do this.

Getting yet another fee, clearly excited Sabro. Her big grin clearly showed her wrinkles, which looked like deep woodcuts by a nonskilled carver.

Whenever Sabro came to visit this family, she would always bring a gift from her village for Roya, Safia's daughter.

"I have something for Roya Jan," she said, and from her satchel, she took out a tiny vest and showed it to Safia. "A beautiful small vest. Roya will love to show it at the handiworks show at school." Safia admired its exquisite workmanship, and then asked her to put it on the shelf for safekeeping.

Sabro thought, *These city people with all the expensive things they have, still admire a simple thing from a village! However, I will get my money!* Seeing Safia's interest, Sabro gave her the other vest too, which had a different color and design.

A lot of attention was being given to these vests. Sabro started to place them on the shelf next to her. She soon realized that they were heavier than what she had expected. She then used her hands as scales, trying to determine why those vests were heavier than the other village vests. *They might be stuffed with more cotton*, she reasoned. *But who cares? Roya loves everything I bring from the village*, she thought. She then placed the vests on the shelf for safekeeping.

Before Sabro left, she said, "I am going to spend the night with Shreen and tomorrow morning I will bring you the other baby girl."

Safia, as usual, gave her some money for the return trip, and the old cook handed her some food, tea, sugar, a few boxes of matches, soaps, and some other items that she put in her large satchel.

On her way through Kabul, she stopped at the street market and bought a few things for her daughter, who was very poor. She then remembered the babies' prayer charms and thought about Ozra who always came to visit Safia. She now feared that Ozra might recognize the charms and find out who the baby was.

The charm will reveal that the child belongs to Niki, and I forgot to take it off, she thought and stopped walking to think what to do. She remembered that she was coming back tomorrow to bring the other baby.

"Tomorrow, when I come back, I will then make up an excuse and take the charm from the baby's neck, she thought. She became mad at herself, but then she felt better that it was not really her fault since her original plan was to leave the babies on the steps of the faraway mosque to begin with.

Then the unthinkable happened. While she was crossing the wide street heading to the bus stop, a speeding car hit her. The driver did not stop. She fell into the street with blood running out from under her burqa, and all the items in her satchel were strewn over the street.

The bus driver's assistant joined the curious onlookers and recognized the woman.

***

Darkness came, and Shah Gul was still waiting for Sabro, blaming herself for not requesting her to come directly home after leaving the babies at the mosque: "Probably went to visit her daughter or her son, stupid woman!"

It was very late when Hajji Khan and Zalmai returned home from the hospital. Shah Gul had waited up for them and they told her about Niki's worsening condition.

With a firm tone, Shah Gul responded, "The babies were sick too—they died!"

"Died?" both father and son asked. Their voices were filled with sorrow. They never had a chance to see the babies.

"Were they very sick? And what did you do?" her husband asked with surprise.

Shah Gul, in a sad and dramatic fashion, said, "Sabro helped. She took them to the cemetery."

Her husband furiously asked, "Did you call the village *mullah*? You should have waited for us. They were not *haramies* to be merely sent straight to the graves."

Shah Gul said, "The person working at the cemetery did everything for the newborn babies. Babies are fragile. When I saw them so sick, I was about to send someone to get a car to take them to the hospital too. They died, and we can't keep dead bodies for hours."

After a few minutes' pause, her husband said, "You're right. You can't keep them all day long. This was probably their destiny, to die while they were babies. Soon I will go and fix their graves. They were my grandchildren!"

"When Niki comes home, we will then have a memorial service for them," Shah Gul said.

In a short while, Sabro's husband and daughter came to the house. From the hall, the daughter who was crying loudly said, "Aunt Shah Gul, they brought the dead body of my mother."

As it was usual in the villages, the servants called the lady of the house Aunt for respect. In the cities, they call them Bibi or Khanoum, meaning "madame."

Both Hajji Khan and Shah Gul hurriedly ran out of their bedroom to see what was happening.

The young girl said, "A car hit my mother, and they brought her dead body back to the village."

Shah Gul sympathized with the girl, gave her comfort, and then sent her home. The next day, Hajji Khan went to the hospital and informed his son and Niki's mother about Sabro's accident.

Shah Gul then thought, *Probably, after she placed the babies on the porch of the mosque she directly went to Kabul. She always did this. When I sent her to do something for me outside of the house, she stopped many times at her relatives' or her married children's houses, or she went to Kabul.*

The next day, Hajji Khan went to the hospital, and informed his son and Niki's mother about Sabro's accident. Later that same day, Niki's condition stabilized, and she then asked about her babies. Her mother slowly began talking about how fragile new babies are, and if they are sick all the time, they will be handicapped. She finally told Niki that her twin girls were dead.

Niki's eyes went dark, and she started to weep.

Chapter 11

Three days passed while Safia, Khadija, and Roya waited anxiously for Sabro to bring the other twin sister to them; however, there was no sign of her.

"Something must have happened to her, otherwise she would definitely have come to get her money for the baby she brought us," Safia said.

"And Roya added, I also have some money to pay her for the two vests she brought us." I love them, and I will take them to the handiworks show in my school."

That day, Safia sent the old cook to Angur Dara Village to see why Sabro had not come back to Kabul. The old cook returned with the sad news that Sabro was dead.

The women were upset at losing the faithful daughter of their parents' gardener.

Safia told the old cook, "Take a taxi and go to Shreen's house in Sheen Ghala and listen to me carefully. Shreen has a baby girl that Sabro was supposed to bring to me. Take this money with you to give her. Keep these extra five hundred Afghanis with you if she asks for more, and bring me the baby. Shreen does not want a baby girl. The girl is an orphan."

The old cook went to Shreen's house. Safia, Khadija, and Roya were anxiously awaiting the other baby's arrival and talked incessantly about it.

Roya said, "I hope they are identical twins. It would be fun to have two girls with the same face."

They decided that Safia would adopt the other baby girl.

"What will we name this baby girl?" Roya asked.

"Your Aunt Khadija has a long list of names. We will pick one," Safia said.

"Aunt Khadija, let's name this one Yasameen," Roya said.

"It is a beautiful name, and it is also on the top of my list," Khadija said.

All of them agreed to name the baby girl Yasameen.

Habib, Safia's husband, who was reading a newspaper, while also listening to the women's conversation, put his newspaper down and asked, "When the other baby girl arrives, then as a father, do I have a right to choose a name for her?"

"Yes, tell us your favorite name?" All three women asked.

"Sofia," he said.

"Good choice, since we knew that you like Sofia Loren," the women said.

He defended himself, "No, it is similar to Safia, my lovely wife's name. However, I like seeing Sofia Loren in the movies, and she is very successful."

They talked about a*shabeshash* for the girl, which was common in Kabul, to celebrate the birth of a girl, as well as a boy.

The old cook finally returned. When the doorbell rang, and the servant boy ran to open the gate, everybody in the living room ran outside. The old cook entered empty-handed with the sad news that yesterday Shreen had sold the baby girl for two hundred Afghanis to a beggar woman in Kabul.

He said, "I asked Shreen where the beggar woman lived. She described the woman's address. The old cook knows the place, which is the poorest area in Kabul."

The old cook confidently headed to find the woman's house to complete his mission—to bring the baby girl to her new home.

He found the beggar woman's house, told her the reason for his visit, and offered her some money. The woman told him that she had sold the girl to the head of the beggars, Pahlawan. The beggar woman said if the old cook gave her more money, she would show him Pahlawan's house. The old cook gave her more money, and the woman accompanied him to Pahlawan's house, not too far from her house.

The woman knocked on the rough wooden door of the house, which was located in a darken part of a dirty alley. A tall man opened the door. The woman entered and the door was closed behind her.

The old cook heard the man shouting at her and cursing her, "Stupid bitch, didn't I tell you not to bring people near my house?"

"There is no danger from his side. He is looking for the little girl that I sold you last night. He is looking for adoption, and he looks rich. In exchange for that tiny little baby for whom you still have to buy milk to feed, you may get lots of money," the woman said.

"You are still a stupid bitch. Let's go and talk with that old man," he said.

The old cook who heard them told himself, "Both of them are stupid because I heard them."

Pahlawan said, "Brother, this woman said that you want that baby girl for adoption. Unfortunately, my sister, who cannot have a child, has always asked the neighbors to find her an orphan child. Finally, this woman found her one. If you want her, then you have to pay some money for my sister to get herself another one. Give me two thousand Afghanis, and I will bring her here tomorrow."

The old cook said, "I have only one thousand on me. Give me the girl, and I will bring the rest of the money tomorrow."

The man demanded, "Give me the one thousand as a down payment, and tomorrow bring another thousand and take the baby. She is at my sister's house. I have to bring her here."

The old cook gave him the one thousand Afghanis and left.

Early the next morning, the cook went back to Pahlawan's house with another thousand Afghanis in his pocket. Near Pahlawan's house, he saw several women with tattered burqas walking through the dirty alley to the big street. All of them were carrying children. The children were of different ages. He went straight to Pahlawan's house and knocked on the door. A young woman opened the door, without any veil, looking disturbed by the knock on her door, and stood directly in front of the cook.

The old cook said, "Sister, I am looking for Pahlawan. I have something for him."

"No one by this name lives here and don't knock that hard on people's houses," the woman harshly said, slamming the door in his face and putting the latch on.

The disturbed cook did not dare knock again. He went toward the small shops, across the dirty alley, and asked one of the shopkeepers about Pahlawan. The shopkeeper, an older man, said, "I don't know this name. That alley is getting more mysterious with all those professional beggars. Every morning, they carry out children to the streets to beg. They put fake bandages on their heads, feet, and the rest of their bodies and drug them to keep them asleep for many hours. Unfortunately, the police are with them! Once, with the other shopkeepers, we complained to the police, and they fined us for unknown reasons. We have families to feed. We see things, we suffer, but we cannot do a thing. We are powerless."

The old cook said good-bye to the old man and ran toward the house of the woman who had brought him yesterday to Pahlawan's door. When he saw her, he told her that Pahlawan was not there.

The woman went inside her house to pick up her burqa, and then she walked with the old cook to the dirty alley. When they reached Pahlawan's house, the woman knocked on the door next to the one that she knocked on yesterday. The old cook felt confused.

A man came out and asked the woman what she wanted. The woman asked about Pahlawan.

"His lease was up yesterday, and he moved out early in the morning," the man said.

"Brother, I don't know how to help you," the woman said to the old cook and walked away.

The old cook stood wondering. He wanted to do something for Safia's family because they were very kind to him and his family. This was a good opportunity to show them his faithfulness. Unfortunately, he returned home empty-handed, disappointed that he was not able to complete his mission. In addition, he had been fooled. He told the sad story to the women of the house.

When Safia, Khadija, and Roya heard about the strange things going on in Kabul, they felt sorry for the missing baby girl in the hand of beggars and wished one day to find her.

"We will keep searching to save that sweet innocent baby girl," Safia said and the other two agreed. "Look at the destiny of that poor newborn baby. Instead of being in her mother's warm arms, she is now in the cold, ruthless hands of beggars," Safia lamented.

Chapter 12

While caring for Niki the last few days, everybody forgot that she had been breastfeeding her babies and, in addition, that Amira had fed them with goat's milk. While she was in the hospital, her milk ducts clogged and became inflamed, making her exhausted and leading to breast infections. A nurse, with the help of Niki's mother, tried the traditional midwife's ways: putting hot herbs on her breasts, using medication to reduce the pain and gradually pumping the milk out. She suffered until the milk finally dried up.

However, Niki's general health condition was worsening, and doctors in the Wazir Akbar Khan Hospital advised the family to rush her to a hospital in Pakistan.

Nur Gul found a people-smuggler who would take them to Peshawar for ten thousand Afghanis per person. They were supposed to leave that day at 4:00 p.m.

It was early morning, and Niki was still asleep because of the medication. Ozra told Nur Gul, "I am going to Safia's house, which is not far from here, to tell her that Niki is very sick and we are leaving today to Peshawar. You know that Niki is like a daughter to her," she emphasized.

Nur Gul brought a taxi and said something to the driver, then turned to Ozra. "Aunt, the taxi driver will take you and bring you back."

At her relatives' house, Ozra told Safia that Niki was in the hospital, and the doctors had advised taking her to a hospital in Pakistan, as soon as possible. "And we will leave today around 4:00 p.m." Ozra said

Safia became very worried for her Niki and decided to go to the hospital with Ozra.

As Safia was leaving, a tall, skinny nanny, who was holding a tiny well-clothed baby, entered the room and said, "Salaam."

Ozra responded, "Salaam." And she asked, "Whose baby is she? And what is her name?"

The nanny answered, "Bibi Khadija's baby. Her name is Yasameen."

Ozra thought, "So wonderful that Khadija found a child." She knew that Khadija could not have a baby on her own. Then she held the baby, kissed her forehead, recited a short verse from the Holy Qur'an, and started to walk around the room, while still holding the baby. She stopped in front of a shelf where she noticed two little village-style vests, one green and other golden, the style she knew how to make.

Ozra thought, *Niki probably made these for Khadija Jan's baby girl and sent them to her.*

From the hallway, Safia called, "I am ready."

Both women got into the taxi and headed to see Niki. Being from the city, Safia was dressed European style, with a jacket and skirt, stockings with high heels, and carried a black leather purse. Ozra, from the village, was covered head to toe in a traditional dark blue burqa.

In the taxi, Ozra said, "Very good news for Khadija's daughter. Nobody told me that she found a baby." Then she frowned a little and said, "If I had known, then I would have embroidered a beautiful quilt cover for the baby's crib, like I did for your other children."

"This happened a few days ago. You could still make her what you want. The girl also has a twin who is missing. Now, tell me about Niki," Safia asked.

Ozra, greatly alarmed at what she just heard about a missing twin, whispered to Safia, "I will tell you about Niki in the hospital. It is a long story. It is very embarrassing, but you have to hear it from me."

Both women arrived at the hospital and went to Niki's room. She was awake, and Nur Gul was sitting next to her. He got up, greeted the women and gave his seat to Safia. When Niki saw Aunt Safia, she smiled, and her beautiful eyes opened widely. Safia gently kissed her on the cheek and began to quietly recite a few verses of the Holy Qur'an. With those calming words her eyes softly closed and she fell asleep.

While Niki slept, the two women walked to the waiting room to update each other on the latest news.

"Now, tell me about Niki, what happened to her?" Safia asked.

"Niki became pregnant in my house! Shah Gul learned about it, came to my house, and took her home, claimed that Nur Gul and Niki already performed the *nikah* and there is no need for the wedding. People thought that because of the war the big wedding was cancelled," Ozra said, and added, "During the past two months, I was disappointed and embarrassed and did not go out of the house. And did not know what was going on with Niki."

She began to cry and said, "I was not welcome in Shah Gul's house. When Niki gave birth, they did not even send for me." She now wept even more and couldn't continue. She never told Safia that Niki had delivered twins. Ozra, however, didn't know that Niki had stayed at Amira's house, and not at Shah Gul's.

"My greatest happiness is that Nur Gul supports Niki, but she is still very sick," Ozra said, as tears came to Amira's eyes, as well. They both now cried together.

Safia's heart pained to see Niki so sick, weak, and gaunt, "Poor girl, poor girl." Then she said, "It is a good idea to take her to Pakistan. They have good hospitals," she said.

Safia then added, "You know that my sister, Khadija, had always asked people to find her a child. Finally, she found that orphan baby."

At no time did Safia mention Sabro's name. The two women had no idea that their conversations were connected. They were totally focused on Niki's declining condition.

Later Roya came with her father, Habib, to the hospital. He spoke with one of the doctors. The doctor told him that Niki had internal bleeding, her lungs and her kidneys were damaged, and he was not sure if it was from giving birth to twins or from somebody beating her up, badly, as it seemed.

The doctor added, "For treatment, my team advised them to take her, as soon as possible, to Pakistan. Their hospitals have the best specialists and equipment, along with the right medicine that she needs. Our hospital is not like before. During the war, we lost our doctors. Our equipment does not function, and medications are hard to find."

Habib told Safia about Niki's condition. She replied, "It is good to take her to Pakistan." Both of them offered their help to Ozra and Nur Gul. Safia made a list of what Ozra and Niki needed and gave it to Roya to go and buy. She emphasized to make it fast and not to be late.

They all were in the waiting room when Yaqub Khan, with Amira and Robia, came to the hospital and joined them. Yaqub Khan greeted the women and went to sit with Nur Gul and Habib on the other side of the room.

Roya's father spoke with Nur Gul, giving him the address of a well-known hospital in Peshawar. He handed him his phone number to call with updates on Niki's condition. Hajji Khan and Zalmai then left to go purchase the necessary items that Nur Gul would need for the trip.

When Roya returned from buying needed things for Ozra and Niki, she met Robia in the hospital. They sat with each other and worried together about their ailing friend.

"Niki talked about you all the time," said Robia.

"We were like two sisters, one in the city and one in the village," Roya said.

Just before 4:00 p.m. that afternoon the paid smuggler came to pick them up. Nur Gul was anxious to get going, but the dust coated old car needed to be loaded. Hajji Khan and Zalmai finally showed up with bags for Niki and Ozra. Zalmai placed them in the trunk, while Nur Gul carried his frail wife to the car. He carefully placed her in the back seat where she now rested her weary head on her mother's shoulder. Nur Gul took his seat in front with the driver. Before the door could close, Roya and Robia approached their helpless friend. Each leaned into the car and kissed Niki's sunken cheeks, and said their goodbyes. They then joined the other family members silently standing outside the hospital and they all watched with saddened hearts as the four sped off to Peshawar.

They traveled all night through the long valley of the steep Hindu Kush Mountains. In the dark, everything looked black and gray, and the beautiful valley where the blue-colored waters of the Kabul River flowed could not be seen. With the approaching dawn you could begin to see the small waterfalls trinkling down to join the river below. The mountain rocks changed colors many times and the different varieties of wild flowers, plants and trees were becoming visible near the mountain streams.

Along the way they made several short stops at roadside cafes to eat and refresh themselves. Their longest stop was at the Torkham's checkpoint at the border. The smuggler first went to the Afghan checkpoint, then to the Pakistan one, to get a travel pass and pay the road fee. He handed the border guard a large bribe, knowing what was required.

Shortly after dawn, they reached the Khyber Pass and was now in a very harsh and unsafe moutainous region. The tall walled houses in this area looked like prisons. The few who traveled these roads had to be very cautious and vigilant. However, in spite of the dangers and perils of this region, the journey was peaceful.

Finally, they reached Peshawar and the car stopped in front of the hospital that was suggested to Nur Gul. All the way, Niki had been in and out of consciousness.

When checking Niki into the hospital, Nur Gul asked for the best room for her. The hospital's officials, who saw a rich Afghan man who could afford to pay for the best and most expensive hospital in the city, welcomed them and immediately started to treat Niki. Nur Gul remembered Yaqub Khan's advice to pay the doctors well, and giving good tips to the nurses and the other hospital workers would also help.

In the next few days, Niki was able to open her eyes and eat. As soon as she started to talk, she talked about Aunt Amira, Uncle Yaqub, Robia, Nur Gul, and her babies and said, "Mother, when I get a little strength, I will tell you about the kindness of Aunt Amira, Uncle Yaqub Khan, Robia, and Nur Gul, and the treasure we found."

Ozra was overjoyed seeing her daughter feeling better and listened to her attentively. Niki kept talking, "Mother, I wish you had seen my twin babies, they were like beautiful dolls. Aunt Amira and I made them vests. One was green, and the other was a golden color.

I remembered the design of the one you made for me that you kept in your trunk as a childhood souvenir." After a short silence, she surprised her mother and said, "Oh, Aunt Amira sewed some of my precious stones and gold coins inside those two vests!"

Ozra said to herself, "Niki's precious stones and gold coins? She must be hallucinating. I am sure that her mother-in-law did not give her even a copper ring, but here she talks about precious stones and gold coins."

This time, the nurse came in with sweet mixed milk and tea called *dudpaty*, a popular Pakistani hot drink.

Niki started to sip the soothing drink, and now only wanted to talk with her mother about the good times. Ozra, however, was still trying to understand everything and connect it all together.

Being heavily medicated Niki soon fell asleep, but Ozra remained wide awake still trying to make some sense out of all that had happened. She thought about the twin baby girls, and the two vests on Safia's shelves.

Ozra kept trying to make some sense from all of this.

Later, when Nur Gul came, she asked him for Roya's father's phone number.

Nur Gul searched his pockets. From one of them, he took out many small pieces of paper, picked out one of them, and gave it to her. Ozra left the room and went to the nurses' station.

There is no need for more thinking. By asking only two questions, I will know what Niki is trying to tell me, she told herself.

For a moment, she changed her mind to call Kabul, thinking, *Niki might be telling these things because of her fever. But my heart is saying that something happened to Niki and her baby girls. I saw those vests, exactly the same color as Niki described.*

She walked to the nurses' station and looked for the nurse who had helped them during the past few days. The nurse had received many tips. The nurse saw Ozra and, with a smile, came to her.

Ozra, in Pashto, told her what she wanted and gave her the phone number.

The nurse took her to a room on the second floor where there was a phone on the table. The nurse picked up the phone, dialed the operator, and gave her the number.

When Safia answered, the nurse handed the phone to Ozra.

In front of the nurse, Ozra spoke in Farsi to her relative in Kabul, "Sister Safia, how are you and the family? Niki is fine. My dear, I have to find out something. Please before asking me any questions, tell me . . . who brought the baby to you?"

"Sabro," Safia said.

"Sabro!" Ozra with a surprised voice said, then asked her a favor. "Sister, go get one of those vests on your living room shelf and tear it open. If there is something inside it, then I will tell you something important about Khadija's baby."

The nurse, who did not know how to speak Farsi, stood quietly at a distance. Ozra impatiently waited for Safia's return. At that moment, the phone cut off.

Ozra waited for the nurse to connect her again. Meanwhile, in her mind she said, *Sabro, Shah Gul's servant! When they said the girls were dead, I could not believe it.*

On the other end, Safia was looking for the vests but did not see them on the shelves and then ran to Roya's room. There she saw them on her desk. She cut one of them apart and gasped to see the coins and colorful stones sewn inside it.

Safia, overcome by what she saw, ran to the living room to answer Ozra. The phone was still not working. The line connected and disconnected several times. Finally, it remained connected and Safia said, "The things you spoke of were inside the vest!" Then the women told each other what they knew about the twins, including that Sabro had brought the baby girl to Khadija, telling her that the twins are orphans. Ozra remembered that her daughter had said that Amira and Robia helped her with the babies.

"Amira and Robia could verify if Khadija's new baby is one of the twins," Ozra said.

"First ask the nurse to give me the phone number of the hospital so that I can call you. I am going to see Amira and Robia without wasting any time," Safia said. She was anxious to know the identity of the baby and the mystery of the jewels in the vests.

Ozra asked the nurse to give the hospital's number to Safia. The Pakistani nurse, in English, gave her the number.

Later that night, the nurse came and told Ozra that there was a phone call for her from Kabul. Ozra went with the nurse to get the call.

Safia was on the phone. "We have one of Niki's babies! We went to visit Amira and Robia and took the baby with us. They were surprised, shocked, and happy to see the baby with us. The baby has one of the prayer charms which Amira had for her daughters and had given to the babies."

Both women promised to keep this information beween themselves until they knew what actually happened. For now, they wanted to tell Niki and Nur Gul that Khadija has one of her babies, and she will be safe, and that it was Sabro who had taken the baby to her.

Ozra quickly went to Niki's room and even though she was sound asleep, woke her up to share the good news with her.

"I am sure that my mother-in-law asked Sabro to give the babies away, and Sabro did a good job taking one of them to Aunt Khadija. At least one of my babies is alive and safe," Niki said. She took a long breath then said, "Ask Aunt Safia to give some money to Sabro, and she will tell her everything. And also about the other baby."

"Sabro is dead, a car hit her in Kabul," Ozra said.

"God bless her soul, even though she was always very cold to me. During the two months when I was there, she did not speak one word to me, showing her faithfulness to my mother-in-law. However, I am very grateful that at the end she did something so incredibly good for me," Niki said.

Ozra, surprised by seeing Nur Gul so indifferent about the babies, thought, *But they were Nur Gul's children too! Why would Shah Gul give them away?* She became angry at Shah Gul, and thought to herself, *As soon as I get back to Afghanistan, I will go to her and ask what she did to the babies—and why. Now it is not the time. My daughter is very ill. I better keep quiet*, she told herself.

The nurse activated the phone in Niki's private room. Later that evening while Nur Gul was there, the phone rang and he answered it. Safia was calling for Niki. He quickly turned the phone over to her. Safia told Niki not to worry about the baby and the vests, and that she will keep them safe until she returned.

Niki in a low and weakened voice said, "Aunt, from the bottom of my heart, I give my baby to Aunt Khadija, my babe is so fortunate to be raised by her. About the vests, everything inside them belongs to me. Nur Gul knows about it. Now, give one of them to Aunt Khadija and the other one to Roya, as a souvenir from me."

She added with great emphasis, "The things inside them are real. I will tell my mother more about them so she can tell you. Do not mention it to strangers, as I was told, for our safety."

After a moment's pause, she said, "I tried to tell my mother about those vests, but she looked at me like I had a fever. I love you very much." With a happy heart she handed the phone back to her husband.

Niki felt sad about the other baby and what happened to her. *Probably she died*, she thought and she also felt, *This is the perfect solution for the other one who is alive. Thanks to Allah that Aunt Khadija has my baby! This was beyond my wish.* She was at peace. Looking at Nur Gul, it seemed that he was at peace too.

Ozra was deeply surprised by Nur Gul's silence even when he heard about the baby girls.

Nur Gul was certain that his mother had made all the plans about the girls, but he kept quiet and did not want to think about the babies. He was happy to see his wife starting to feel better again.

That evening, he went to see some Afghan refugees who had come earlier to the city to help him rent a house for his family and Uncle Yaqub Khan's family.

On the way back to the hospital, he passed in front of some well-lighted jewelry stores. He stopped at the window of one of them, fascinated by the jewelry glittering under a strong light. He went inside the store and bought a pair of gold earrings for Niki.

When Nur Gul arrived back at the hospital, he privately gave his gift to Niki and asked her to wear them. She loved her first pair of gold earrings, in the little red velvet box, but she asked Nur Gul to place this precious box and its golden treasures under her pillow for the moment because she felt too weak to wear them.

The next morning, Nur Gul went to get some breakfast, and Ozra helped Niki to take a bath. She asked for her new sky blue dress and pants to wear. Then Ozra braided her long date-colored hair.

While her mother braided her hair, Niki told her about the night of her journey to Sheen Klay. At the end, she asked of her mother, "Promise me that you will not mention our findings to anybody. Uncle said it is dangerous if people know about them."

"You have my promise, my lips are sealed," Ozra agreed. What her daughter said sounded like the old tales, and she was anxious to hear more about it. She was thinking about that old caravansary ever since she had heard stories about it. Niki's voice disrupted her thoughts. "Can I wear my earrings?"

"Of course, my dear," Ozra said and helped Niki put them on.

Later that day, the nurse, who was in charge of Niki's care, told the other nurses, "That young Afghan woman looks like a fairy tale princess. Afghan women are beautiful, but she is the most beautiful one I have ever seen. She is very sick but never complains. Unfortunately, her last night's medical reports disappointed the doctors."

Nur Gul returned with breakfast and was very pleased to see his wife dressed up and proudly wearing her gold earrings. "She is very beautiful," he told himself, but was too shy to mention it aloud in front of his mother-in-law.

After breakfast, Ozra left the room. Nur Gul told his beautiful wife about Peshawar's parks, gardens, and the house he had found for them. He promised her that as soon as she feels strong enough, he would take her to those parks, gardens, and show her the house.

That evening, Niki's body badly weakened rejecting the most recent treatment. Wearing the gold earrings, Niki died peacefully, with Nur Gul at her side. Her body was buried in a nearby cemetery, in a grave next to other Afghan refugees who also had sought peace in a foreign land.

The poor girl got engaged at an early age, was raped, and became pregnant, which put the family honor in danger. Her mother-in-law beat her nearly to death and locked her in a stable, where she gave birth to a set of twins. She was saved from death by a neighbor and hidden in that neighbor's house. She became ill soon after birth and died! What has happened to the man who raped her? He is continuing his normal life! Nur Gul was thinking, and his thoughts of taking revenge grew stronger and stronger.

Both families eventually moved to Peshawar. Ozra lived with Amira's family, and as the sun rose every day, she walked to visit Niki's grave.

Throughout this time, Nur Gul could only think of one thing. He had to go back to Afghanistan, find Baz Gul, and have his revenge!

Chapter 13

Yaqub Khan tried to persuade Nur Gul from going back to Afghanistan. Nur Gul trusted Yaqub Khan and told him his big secret: that Baz Gul had raped Niki, and he felt obligated to go to Baghlan to take his revenge.

Yaqub Khan, after hearing Nur Gul, agreed with his decision. Before responding to Nur Gul, though, he rubbed his salt-and-pepper-colored mustache, and with anger said, "My son, let's go get that villain bastard together. In Baghlan, I have a powerful friend from long time ago. If we come across a problem, then I can go and ask for his help. His name is Azer Bey."

Both men immediately left Peshawar.

In those days, travel was not easy because of fighting between the *Mujahedeen* and the Communists. Their destination was far away. Yaqub Khan and Nur Gul could afford to hire a private car and a driver, but because of the security, it made better sense to travel by the public bus, which would be less noticeable

At the first border checkpoint, all the male passengers got off the bus and walked toward a guard who forcefully demanded, "The road fees!"

Previously, the passengers showed their passports or travel documents, and the drivers paid the road fees to the checkpoint guards. Things were changing rapidly. This time, there were no questions about passports or other documents. The guards simply asked for money from each passenger.

Yaqub Khan and Nur Gul noticed that the other passengers had money ready to hand to the guard without exchanging any words. Yaqub Khan asked one of the passengers, "Brother, how much are we supposed to pay?"

The passenger softly said, "There is no fixed rate, these guards will accept what you give them." It seemed they had traveled many times and knew the rules of the road of those days. The passengers paid the bribes, and the bus continued across the border.

The situation at the checkpoint on the Afghan side was far worse. Again, all the male passengers got off the bus to pay the road fee. Two young guards collected the money and insulted the passengers if they paid poorly. Insulting older people was unacceptable. But that was in the past. Now they had no choice but to accept the dishonor and remain silent.

Yaqub Khan took out some money from his pocket to pay for Nur Gul and himself. When it was his turn, the guard grabbed the money, looked at them for a few seconds, and laughing loudly threw the money at Yaqub Khan' face.

"Look at his nice clothes and fine mustache and see how much he paid for two people! Son of a bitch thinks that we are beggars!"

Yaqub Khan was clearly embarrassed by this insult but, humbly from his vest pocket, took out some more money and handed it to the guard.

During the rest of the ride, they had a few other stops similar to the first ones. Nobody on the bus ever dared to ask, "Why should we pay?" They learned all about the killing and beatings at these checkpoints if the passengers did not obey the guards' orders. A few poor men, who were not able to pay, were beaten by the guards, ridiculed, and then allowed to get back on the bus, still alive but disgraced.

The bus finally reached the center of Baghlan. Yaqub Khan and Nur Gul spent the night in its only good hotel.

Yaqub Khan thought, *Nur Gul is too kind and too nice to take revenge and kill.*

He said to Nur Gul, "About Baz Gul, my advice is to not think about killing him and put your own self in trouble. We should give a large bribe to the government officers in charge and talk with the elders who are the real decision makers to have him put in jail for life, where people cannot survive for long." Yaqub Khan added, "We have another obligation to fulfill—join the *Mujahedeen* and fight against our current nonreligious government and the Soviet army, who are looting and killing our people every day without mercy."

"Uncle, you are right. But I want to kill him," Nur Gul said nervously.

Yaqub Khan said, "You have other obligations as I mentioned, and killing Baz Gul will put you in jail. With a bribe, I can release you, but there will be too many problems. Think about something else."

The next day, before dawn, they hired a car from the hotel's owner to take them where Baz Gul lived, which was not far away. Nur Gul had heard many times, from Ozra, about where he lived.

When they reached that small village, it was time for the morning prayers. They went to the mosque.

After the prayers, the *mullah* and the elders welcomed their guests and asked the purpose of their visit.

Yaqub Khan spoke, "Brothers, I am Yaqub, from the Angur Dara Village, near Kabul, and the young man is my nephew. We have come from far away on behalf of one of our relatives who could not come with us."

Yaqub Khan purposely said on behalf of one of our relatives because he did not want to embarrass Nur Gul in front of people in the mosque.

He told them about the heinous crime which was committed by Baz Gul, one of the men living among them. That morning, Baz Gul was not in the mosque, but his elderly father-in-law was.

The elders discussed the matter among each other, cursed Baz Gul, and decided on the spot that giving *bad* would be the solution.

The elders agreed on *bad*, an old Afghan tradition, which is to marry a girl or several girls from the man's family who committed the crime in exchange for revenge.

"We want peace, take Baz Gul's daughter. This is our final decision," the oldest man in the mosque said.

Yaqub Khan was smart not to mention Nur Gul's name, otherwise Nur Gul would have had to accept the proposal of the elders to marry Baz Gul's daughter, and they probably would perform *nikah* right away.

Baz Gul's father-in-law did not speak, but his face reflected the pain of deep grief. As a sign of respect to the elders, he agreed to give his granddaughter as *bad* to the man who had lost his wife, or if he does not marry her, one of his relatives who needs a wife could marry the granddaughter. He was supposed to travel with the girl as her companion.

"Tomorrow we will be ready. Come and pick us up," the old man said solemnly.

The *Bey* of that small Uzbek village, who was among the elders in that mosque, offered his hospitality, as was the usual tradition, and took these Pashtun visitors to his guesthouse.

The next morning, after prayers, a servant of the Uzbek *Bey* took them to the old man's house. The old man walked the two men to a room, which was decently furnished. Yaqub Khan and Nur Gul squatted silently next to each other, facing the old man.

It wasn't long before the old man said, "The girl is ready. I pray and hope that your relative, who is going to marry her, will also take good care of her. Giving *bad* is the hardest punishment for a family, taking away their innocent girl, who did no wrong."

Sadly, the old man dropped his head and shed a few tears, which rolled down his face and disappeared in his thin white beard. He was embarrassed that he had cried in front of the other men.

Then he asked them to follow him to a room at the end of a small dark hall. There, an old woman was lying on a mattress on the ground. A brightly colored quilt covered her body up to her neck. Another female, whose veil covered her face, was sitting next to her. Both women were weeping quietly.

"Get up, my daughter, and say good-bye to your sick mother," the old man said with a trembling voice. The girl with the veil dropped herself on top of her mother, stayed in that position for a few seconds, and let out a loud cry. Then she stood. Her veil fell from her face. She hurriedly grabbed it and greeted the guests.

Yaqub Khan and Nur Gul were surprised to see the older girl, and they both noticed that one of her front teeth was missing.

The old man begged, "Please have mercy on us and do not take her away. Baz Gul is a coward, and he is not a responsible father. If you take her away or not, it will make no difference to him. For sure, it will break our hearts."

Both Yaqub Khan and Nur Gul whispered to each other, "The elders at the mosque were talking about giving as *bad* Baz Gul's daughter, not his wife,"

After a pause, the old man continued, "My sons, if you are looking for revenge, then listen to me: bribe the government officers. They will put Baz Gul in the horrible jail of this town where the prisoners do not last long. They die in dark cells full of dirt, insects, and from having not enough food."

"We need a few moments," Yaqub Khan said to the old man. They left and returned to the previous room.

After seeing the old girl, for a moment they forgot their mission "to punish Baz Gul.'"

"Uncle, let's run away," Nur Gul jokingly said to Yaqub Khan, who was in deep thought.

"See, son, the old man gave the same advice as I told you, to put Baz Gul in jail for life. *Bad* is not working for us, nobody will marry an old girl, and we will end up having an extra load on our shoulders," Yaqub Khan said. And this time, he replied to Nur Gul's joke, "Unless you marry her!" Both men laughed.

The old man also returned to the room. Yaqub Khan asked him to take them to the governor's office. The old man happily left the room to get ready to go with them.

Waiting for the old man, Nur Gul went to the window. From there, he saw two young girls, both wearing skullcaps, the traditional Uzbek hat. Their long hair, in many strands of braids, Uzbek style, were swinging on their backs. The girls raced toward the kitchen with a tall chimney on its roof on the other side of the courtyard.

"Uncle, come and see," Nur Gul said to Yaqub Khan. They saw the girls and kept quiet. They realized that what they had seen earlier was a made-up scene.

However, Nur Gul did not have any desire to marry Baz Gul's daughter. They kept their decision to go with the plan that the old man had suggested.

They went to the governor's building, where the officer in charge came to speak with them. Yaqub Khan offered him a very large bribe to put Baz Gul in jail for life.

Seeing the amount he was being offered he immediately accepted the bribe and said, "The money would not be a bribe because I have to pay to get people to cooperate. I do this to pay respect to you as the guests in this town and to punish the bad man."

Yaqub Khan agreed to pay the large bribe amount to ensure fast action.

The next day, a guard came to take them to the officer in charge. He told them that they had arrested Baz Gul, kept him in a detention room, and that they would soon transfer him to the central prison of Baghlan, known to be one of the worst prisons to be jailed. The officer, who had been clearly impressed with the bribe, offered Yaqub Khan and Nur Gul green tea with *nabat,* the special hard candy found in the north, along with cake.

After a few sips of tea, Nur Gul asked if he could go to see Baz Gul. The officer asked the armed guard to accompany him. On the way, Nur Gul asked the guard if he could be allowed to beat Baz Gul—even to death—if he wanted. The guard quickly agreed after also being handed a good bribe amount. Nur Gul was now ready for his own personal revenge.

When they reached the door of the detention room, Nur Gul could see Baz Gul's big and filthy body through the small barred opening, slumped against the back wall.

He is too big to fight, Nur Gul thought. *Beating him would be like striking my fists into the solid prison walls.*

Nur Gul now wished he had not listened to Yaqub Khan and had brought a gun with him.

A low-ranking prison official unlocked the heavy door at the guard's request. Before entering the small room, Nur Gul quietly had some words with the guard. Fortunately for Nur Gul, the guard was just as big as Baz Gul.

They both entered the room. The guard, without any hesitation, rushed to Baz Gul and started beating him with the butt end of his rifle. The strokes were sudden and unrelenting, one after another, and soon Baz Gul fell to the floor, blood covering his beaten face and body. From the prison floor, Baz Gul saw Nur Gul next to the guard and recognized him but showed no reaction.

Nur Gul spat at him and then thought. *"Just spit at him? I am more cowered than he is. Now it is too late to hit a man who is already fallen to the ground."*

Then the guard started to curse Baz Gul and said, "You did a crime toward a girl and then came to hide among us Uzbeks? You think we will let you stay here and live free? I myself will make your life hell. They will take your daughter as *bad*."

After Baz Gul heard the guard's insults, he slowly lifted his body and, using the wall as support, got up off the ground, all the while keeping his eyes directly at Nur Gul. In an instant, Baz Gul rushed crazily toward him. Nur Gul quickly moved to the side to evade a direct assault by the charging madman. Nur Gul took advantage of that moment and began striking Baz Gul hard with all his strength with his fists. He was able to grab the guard's rifle and continued beating Baz Gul with it, like the guard had done before.

Baz Gul was clearly stunned. Nur Gul could not believe his own strength. Baz Gul, a giant of a man, fell again to the floor.

The guard asked, "I can finish him if you want . . ."

"All his body is broken. Let him suffer in jail," Nur Gul said and then again spat at him, being now all the more contented to do so.

When leaving the bloodied room, the guard respectfully returned the bribe back to Nur Gul, but Nur Gul saw that he was poor and insisted that he accept the bribe as a gift. Nur Gul, being fully satisfied with Baz Gul's punishment, now paid the guard even more.

Nur Gul returned to the office where Yaqub Khan was waiting for him. Both men thanked the officer in charge and told him that they will tell the people in the mosque about their decision of putting Baz Gul in jail instead of getting *bad*. Then they would return to Pakistan.

That night, when the officer in charge went to the mosque, he heard a different story: that the Pashtun men had visited Baz Gul. Baz Gul convinced them that their story was a conspiracy by Ozra, his second wife, because he had returned to his first wife and their daughters. Ozra wanted revenge and made up a story. Baz Gul had never committed any harm to the girl. Therefore, they did not take Baz Gul's daughter as *bad*. Both Pashtun men would return to Pakistan, and they vowed to punish Ozra for her lie.

The old Uzbek father-in-law, who liked his son-in-law, insisted that Baz Gul was a victim and should not be in jail. The officer in charge, who had already received his large bribe, knew his guests were returning soon to Pakistan, far away from Baqhlan, and did not want the resentment of the elders of his village. He agreed to let Baz Gul go free.

Yaqub Khan, before returning to Pakistan, wanted to visit his old friend Azer Bey whom he had already mentioned to Nur Gul. He lived in an expensive part of Baghlan. Both men traveled quite a distance. Finally, they reached the fortress of Azer Bey, on top of a low hill called Zardtapa. The hill was barren and had a dark yellow color. Zardtapa, meaning yellow hill, was surrounded by scorched cotton fields.

At the gate, Yaqub Khan gave his name to the guard. The guard went inside and soon, a short heavyset man with Mongolian features and a long, thin beard came to the gate. The men greeted and hugged each other warmly. Azer Bey shook hands with Nur Gul. They all went to his guest house.

The lunch was a typical Uzbek food: dumplings such as *ashak* and *manto*, chicken and lamb kebabs, golden rice with carrots and raisins, round breads, yogurt, and fruits. Showing off with a variety of foods has always been a custom of the heads of tribes. As usual, a few close friends and relatives of the Bey were in the guest room to join them for lunch.

After lunch, Yaqub Khan and Azer Bey, to catch up with each other's news, went to the other room. Both men were prosperous and had lived comfortable lives until recently. Now they lived in fear of the Communist government, which had started looting, killing, and kidnapping girls and boys. Confiscation of lands had reached many provinces, and many heads of tribes either had been killed or had taken refuge in neighboring countries.

The visit from these two guests, who were living in Peshawar, was good news for the Azer Bey. He insisted on keeping them overnight. The Bey learned more about Yaqub Khan and that Nur Gul was the son of a Khan too, and they were now settled in Peshawar. Both owned businesses, including a large food market.

Chapter 14

The next day, Azer Bey took his guests to the Friday prayers, which many people were attending. People had great respect for Azer Bey, not only because he was the head of his tribe, but because he had been helping his people with food and shelter; and he also financially supported the mosque.

On that day, the *mullah*'s preaching was about finding husbands for their young girls and young widows before the Communist agents could steal them away. He encouraged his people to leave for Iran, Turkey, or Pakistan, and to join the *Mujahedeen*. He emphasized that they should do what he said before the looting and cruelty reached them.

"Looks like the *mullah* read my mind," Azer Bey told himself. Last night, talking with Yaqub, he had an idea.

At the end of the prayers, the Uzbek Bey said that he had an announcement. The crowd carefully listened to him. "I have two guests of honor from far away, and I have decided to marry my sister to Yaqub Khan, and my daughter to Nur Gul."

Yaqub Khan and Nur Gul were totally surprised at Azer Bey's unexpected announcement. They were in shock and didn't know what to say. Yaqub Khan had a great love for Amira and never wanted to have a second wife. Nur Gul was still grieving over Niki's death.

Soon they returned to reality when people surrounded them to congratulate them both.

Another old Afghan tradition to keep one's honor and pride was to accept a marriage offer without any condition; otherwise, one would be considered a coward. It was considered an honor that a friend should offer his daughter or sister to a friend or relative for marriage.

Yaqub Khan and Nur Gul, to show that they were men of honor, both expressed their consent without hesitation and even kissed Azer Bey's hands, as as a future in-law.

That night, the *mullah* came to Azer Bey's home to perform *nikah*. A small group of guests attended the ceremony, and afterwards, a dinner was served. They feasted on a lamb roast with many other side dishes and servings of sweets and tea. Azer Bey could throw large parties with a snap of his finger.

The mother and the old grandmother gave the brides their expensive wedding dresses, hats, and jewelries—which they saved for them—as was the tradition. An aunt, whose husband had a business in Tajikistan, brought many gifts, inclucing Russian *eau de colognes*. She opened one large green bottle and splashed it on the brides' shawls. The strong odor of Russian colognes filled the air and lingered for a while.

Both brides were weeping nonstop, and their friends were whispering to each other: "Poor girls now have broken hearts because they love other men from their Uzbek relatives. They had no choice but to marry these Pashtun men, to be safe and save the family."

A woman relative put henna on the brides' palms and sent some to the grooms to put on their little fingers for good luck and as a sign they were just married. The men were not able to see the girl's faces until they were guided to their bridal rooms.

The Uzbek Bey was very clever, with these marriages, he found rich and good husbands for his sister and his daughter and a place of refuge in Peshawar for himself and family. He had plans to take his large family to Peshawar and then to Turkey. Because of their Uzbek features, they would not fit into Pashtun society in Peshawar, so a marriage connection was the best way to unite the families.

Both Yaqub and Nur Gul returned to Peshawar with the two beautiful Uzbek women. Uzbek girls were well known for their beauty. Nur Gul had no place in his heart for another woman, and Yaqub Khan, had previously cleverly avoided many situations of getting another wife; but in this situation, honor gave him no choice. He was thinking about Amira.

Her husband, not having another wife, had given Amira great feelings of happiness, pride, and stability compared to many other women whose husbands had married more than one wife.

The men returned to Peshawar, and on arriving through the gate, Amira saw the two women with them and initially thought one might be Nur Gul's *bad* and that the other had accompanied her. All these hopes were gone when she noticed Yaqub Khan's little finger colored with henna. Amira now knew he had just married. She tried not to faint.

"Is there any woman in the world fortunate from birth to death? I thought I was going to be that fortunate woman. I have learned in this age that women should accept that our culture reigns over our lives—cruelly," Amira said to herself, and already she felt like "the old wife," thinking about co-wife, stepchildren, fights, and all that goes with being part of such a household.

Amira now further thought, *Sometimes life is going so slow that for many years, nothing special happens, but sometimes, in a short time extraordinary changes occur and with great speed.*

Soon the once radiant Amira turned into a quiet and sad woman. It especially became much harder for her when Yaqub Khan started going to his other wife's room to spend the night. Gifted with a kind heart, she never begrudged the new wife. She knew that the new wife was as much a victim as she was. She treated her as a guest until she became acquainted with her new environment.

Ozra knew that women had been slaves of their culture, and that the Uzbek girl named Sara might not be Nur Gul's only wife forever. Therefore, she convinced Nur Gul to accept the new wife and to be good to her. Ozra told him, "Niki's wish was to see you happy."

Epilogue

In the months after his marriage, Nur Gul slowly began to accept his life without Niki. With the passage of time, he began falling in love with his Uzbek wife, Sara, just as he had done once before with a Pashtun village girl. He still longed, however, for his beautiful Niki.

"I know I must go forward and make a new life with Sara," Nur Gul kept reminding himself, all the while hoping that time would heal his aching heart.

Thoughts of Niki continued to be on Nur Gul's mind. Almost daily, he visited her humble grave, oftentimes bringing the flowers she loved so much—the kind that grew along the stream near the terrace where she and Robia had sewn the babies' vests.

But Ozra visited Niki's grave every day. If they were there together, each would stand silently, side by side, remembering their beloved Niki. Words were rarely exchanged, with just the presence of the other, providing the comfort and healing peace they both were seeking.

Spring soon came, and with it, Nur Gul's life would change. Sara told him she was pregnant. He was overjoyed and while looking into her hazel green eyes that day, he knew there was a request he now needed to make.

The next morning, he walked to Niki's grave. This day not only did he carry a bouquet of sweet-smelling flowers, but also had Sara at his side. On arriving at the cemetery, their eyes were immediately drawn to the sight of a solitary motionless woman standing in the distance. They quietly approached the grieving woman and, without disturbing her downward gaze, joined her silent vigil.

A few moments passed before Nur Gul knelt down and gently placed the flowers on the barren ground. He then looked up, and his eyes met Ozra's. The silence was soon broken. In his usual shy way, with a low and slightly nervous voice, he asked, "If my wife gives birth to a girl, can I have your permission to name her Niki?"

With moistened eyes, he then turned to Sara, and with a strong and proud voice said, "In Pashto and in Farsi, *Niki* means 'goodness.'"

The End

About the Author

Laila was born in Kabul, Afghanistan, a daughter of General Asef Anwarzai the former Commander of the Afghan Royal Air Force. She is a graduate of Malalai High School and Kabul University. As a result of the Soviet invasion of Afghanistan in 1979 her father was imprisoned. In order to avoid imprisonment and persecution themselves, Laila, her husband and their two infant sons, left their homeland for Pakistan. Soon, they were granted political asylum in the United States and settled in New York City before moving to Indianapolis, where their third son was born. Valuing the importance of education, Laila, encouraged by her husband, continued her pursuit of knowledge by earning a Master of Arts from Indiana University, a Master of Science from Martin University, and a Ph.D. from Preston University. This emphasis on education was instilled in her sons, two of whom are now medical doctors and one an attorney. With her sons set on their respective paths, Laila accepted the position of First Secretary of the Afghan Embassy in Islamabad, Pakistan from 2003-2006. She was among one of the first women diplomats appointed by the newly reconstructed Afghanistan government. At the International Women's Conference in Karachi, Pakistan in May 2008 she was honored with the "*International Women's Award*" for her distinguished diplomatic service in difficult and dangerous times. After her tenure abroad, she returned to Indianapolis where she continues to teach, lecture, and write.

CPSIA information can be obtained at www.ICGtesting.com
Printed in the USA
LVOW08s1423100716

495760LV00002BA/343/P